in DUE TIME

STAY A SPELL

by Nicholas O. Time

SIMON SPOTLIGHT

New York   London   Toronto   Sydney   New Delhi

SIMON SPOTLIGHT
An imprint of Simon & Schuster Children's Publishing Division
1230 Avenue of the Americas, New York, New York 10020
This Simon Spotlight hardcover edition July 2016
Copyright © 2016 by Simon & Schuster, Inc.
Text by Sheila Sweeny Higginson. Cover illustration by Stephen Gilpin.
All rights reserved, including the right of reproduction in whole or in part in any form. SIMON SPOTLIGHT and colophon are registered trademarks of Simon & Schuster, Inc. For information about special discounts for bulk purchases, please contact Simon & Schuster Special Sales at 1-866-506-1949 or business@simonandschuster.com.
Designed by Jay Colvin. The text of this book was set in Adobe Garamond Pro.
Manufactured in the United States of America 0516 FFG
10 9 8 7 6 5 4 3 2 1
ISBN 978-1-4814-6727-8 (hc)
ISBN 978-1-4814-6726-1 (pbk)
ISBN 978-1-4814-6728-5 (eBook)
Library of Congress Control Number 2016936491

CHAPTER	TITLE
1	We Are the Change

Did you ever wish you were an octopus? I mean, not in the squishy, looking-like-an undersea-alien kind of way—more like a "you know, having eight arms would be pretty cool right now," feeling. Let me tell you, if I were to see a shooting star, or blow on a dandelion at this very moment, that would be my wish. Jada Reese, girl octopus. I could definitely use at least three more pairs of hands to finish organizing the mess in front of me!

It's my own fault, of course. It always starts

with a brain flash. I see something on the Internet, or I hear a bunch of my friends talking, and this awesome new idea hits me. The problem is, it's usually accompanied by the need to blurt the idea out before I think through all the details.

Like this clothing drive. As soon as I heard that the women's shelter where our teacher Mrs. Donnelly volunteers needed winter clothes, I talked my friends Daniel and Abby into helping me organize an event at our school. I never imagined we would get such a great response from the students at Sands Middle School! Now our cafeteria is filled with boxes and bags stuffed with clothes, and it's my job to make sure they're all organized before they get sent to the shelter.

Don't get me wrong, though. I still think it's a great idea, and totally worth the lunch periods I gave up to organize it. Even better, it involves clothes, which are pretty much my favorite thing on Earth, next to my family and my friends, of course. I just wish I had thought it through a little more first. Maybe rounded up a few hundred extra volunteers, because I'm not sure we're ever going to get all these clothes sorted in time.

"Coats in this pile," I tell Daniel. "Sweaters here, pants over on that table. And shoes and sneakers in this box."

"Yes, sir!" Daniel says, saluting me like I'm a drill sergeant.

I'm totally *not* like a drill sergeant, FYI. I mean, some people, like my little brother, have pointed out my tendency to be somewhat bossy, but they are exaggerating. I just have a very clear idea of what needs to be done. Nothing wrong with that, right?

"Check these out!" Abby calls over, holding up a pair of sparkly flared pants.

"AhhhMAZING!" I gasp.

I can't help but run over and touch them. They're sweet!

"These are so disco!" I cry. "Straight from the seventies!"

"What do you know about the 1970s?" Mrs. Donnelly laughs as she hands me a feathery scarf from the same box.

"Polyester bell-bottoms, platform shoes, wrap dresses." I chuckle when I fling the scarf around my neck. "Mrs. Donnelly, I may have to study for my history tests, but when it comes to fashion, I'm already an expert on every decade!"

"Then I might have to come to you for some fashion tips," Mrs. Donnelly jokes.

"Anytime!" I laugh.

"Seriously, Jada," Mrs. Donnelly continues. "Thank you for giving up your lunch periods to organize this drive. Everyone at the shelter is very grateful."

"Oh, I'm just glad we could help," I tell her. "I've been thinking there's more we can do, like maybe a spring fashion show to raise money?"

"Hold that thought," Mrs. Donnelly says. "It's a good idea, but lunch period is almost over. Make sure to bring it up at our next We Are the Change club meeting."

We Are the Change club. That's another one of my great ideas. I saw a quote on a billboard, supposedly said by Mahatma Gandhi, the Indian leader. It said, "Be the change you wish to see in the world." As soon as I read it, I fell in love with it. It's so me! I want to be the change I wish to see in the world! I knew other kids felt the same way.

So I went to Mrs. Donnelly, who is in charge

of all the school clubs, and she agreed that "We Are the Change" was a great idea for a new club. Daniel and Abby joined right away, because, hello? Best friends. But soon we had more than forty kids coming to our meetings and volunteering at charity events. I knew I wasn't the only one who wanted to be the change!

Then one day, Ms. Tremt, our librarian, gave us a lecture about being accurate in our research, especially on the Internet. I'm sure your teachers have reminded you about it too. Make sure you use accurate, reliable sources. Don't believe everything you read. You know the drill.

Later, I started poking around on my computer and I came across this story about how lots of famous quotes aren't exactly accurate. I decided to find out when exactly Gandhi said that quote. It turns out it's not entirely clear that Gandhi *ever* said those words. Can you believe it? Stupid Internet, making everyone believe things that may or may not be true.

What I did find out, though, was that Gandhi said, "If we could change ourselves, the tendencies in the world would also change. As a man changes his own nature, so does the attitude of the world change toward him. . . . We need not wait to see what others do."

I think it means kind of the same thing—maybe not exactly, but I had already started the club and named it and well, there goes another example to put in my "I should have thought through the details first" list.

So anyway, I take out my planner and jot down a reminder under the tab "We Are the Change." I have to jot down reminders to myself all the time. If I don't, some new big idea will get in the way, and I'll forget to follow through on the big idea I just had. I don't know what I'd do if I ever lost my planner. I guess I'd just have to drag Daniel around with me everywhere—he remembers *everything*! So not fair.

"See you after school?" Abby asks as we pack up our stuff and get ready to head to class.

"Sure, but I have to stop in the library first," I say with a sigh. "Because this."

I hold up my latest spelling test.

Prepare yourself for a shock. I know I sound like I'm pretty together and smart, and I don't mean to brag or be all like, "Hey, check me out. I'm Jada and I'm pretty together and smart." I just know my strengths. But I know my weaknesses, too, and now I am about to reveal my fatal flaw. Can you handle it?

It's spelling. Remember how I said I'm not so great with details? Well, I'm more than not so great with spelling details. I'm horrible. Like a fifty-three-on-my-last-spelling-test horrible. I am shockingly bad at spelling. But hey, I'm lucky enough to live in a time when most of my reports can be typed on my laptop and benefit from spell-check. So how important is spelling really when you get into the real world and don't have to take spelling tests anymore?

"Your evil nemesis," Daniel teases as he does a sinister super-villain sneer. "Spelllllllling."

Of course Daniel only has to look at a word once and he remembers how to spell it. Again, so not fair.

"It's just one test, Jada," Abby says. "You shouldn't be so hard on yourself."

"I'm not," I say. "But it's not just one test, either. So I will be in the library, hitting the spelling books. Even though spelling is my nemesis."

"Okay," Daniel says. "And by the way, that's not spelled 'O' and 'K.'"

"Got it, wise guy." I laugh.

When the bell for last period rings, I head down the hall to the school library. It's become a pretty popular place since Ms. Tremt took over as the school librarian. She seemed a little strange at first, but once you get to know her, she's really interesting and easy to talk to. She also always weirdly seems to know the exact book you're looking for, which I guess is why a copy of *How to Spell Your Way to the T-O-P* is sitting on the table as soon as I walk in.

"Wow, thanks, Ms. Tremt," I whisper to myself, not exactly excited about my new reading material. "How did you know?"

I grab the book and sit down at an empty table. I flip through the pages. It's like torture. Here's the thing about spelling. It doesn't make any sense. Take this rule on page forty-three of *How to Spell Your Way to the T-O-P*:

I before *E*, except after *C* . . . or when sounding like "ay" as in "neighbor" or "weigh."

8

Which makes sense, when you're talking about words like "pie" or "weigh." But then explain to me why W-I-E-R-D is circled in red on my test paper.

None of the other words circled in red on my test make sense to me either. They make my head hurt because they're not logical, the same way "weird" is not logical if you're following the spelling rule on page forty-three.

Algebra I get. There are very few red circles on most of my algebra tests, which is why I'm in the honors class. I know some kids are really struggling with the work we're doing lately, but those problems make sense to me. "Weird" does not. To me, rules are not made to be broken.

I bang my forehead on the book. Maybe the spelling rules will seep in that way. I try to remember Ms. Tremt's words the last time I was looking for some spelling help.

"English is not a logical language, Jada," Ms. Tremt said. "It's made up of many different influences. German, Latin, French, Greek, you name it. There's a smidgen of this and a pinch of that in there. There is not one correct approach to mastering it. You have to stop thinking about it like math."

I don't want to stop thinking about it like math, though. I want it to make sense, or to just go away. As if Ms. Tremt can sense my frustration, just as I slam closed *How to Spell Your Way to the T-O-P*, she appears, magically, in the middle of the library floor, surrounded by boxes of books.

Here is the really w-e-i-r-d thing. I may have been studying, but I definitely didn't hear a door open, or anyone tiptoe into the room. And even if I hadn't heard Ms. Tremt sneak in, there was no way I could have missed Matt, Grace, and Luis, my friends who just happen to somehow suddenly be standing right behind her.

What's even w-e-i-r-d-e-r is that they look like they've stepped out of the movie *Grease*, all decked out in 1950s-style clothes. The saddle shoes and bobby socks that Grace is wearing haven't been in style since my grandmother was in diapers. And Matt is a jock! He would never slick back his hair and wear cuffed jeans. I don't know if I've ever seen him out of his sweatpants.

"Well done, Grace, Luis, and Matt," Ms. Tremt

says, loud enough for everyone in the library to hear. "That is a fabulous magic trick. A very exciting entrance indeed! We'll need to work on it a bit more, but your costumes are perfect for your school project, Fashions Through the Times. Well done!"

The other kids in the library just shake their heads and get back to their books. I can tell they think it's just another wacky Ms. Tremt moment. I disagree. I think it's something bigger than that.

My logical brain is on high alert, so when Ms. Tremt pulls Matt, Grace, and Luis through a door that I never even knew existed before, I quietly follow them and see that they're in a secret, empty classroom. How is it possible that everyone else in the library missed this?

Matt hands Ms. Tremt a shimmering metallic book. She turns right around and says, "Jada? Here's the book we discussed."

The Book of Memories. Ms. Tremt and I did have a discussion about it, a very intense discussion, a couple of days ago. It happened when I noticed her trying to casually sneak the book into a box. The book is way too glitzy to

11

casually sneak anywhere, though. It shimmers kind of like a '70s disco ball.

Ms. Tremt told me that the book was special in ways that I could never imagine, but that she was holding it for someone else first, and when they were done with it, I was next in line. We talked about how reading a book—especially a great one—was like taking a trip through space and time, but how *this* book would take the reader on a trip in bold, new ways.

Those were exactly her words, by the way— "bold, new ways." It sounded like some sci-fi mumbo jumbo, but it also sounded intriguing and exciting the way Ms. Tremt said it. Like it was a secret she couldn't wait to share with me. And I couldn't wait to dive in to it!

Now that it's here, I can hardly believe I'm holding it in my hands.

I smile at Matt and say, "Did you have a nice trip?" Then I give a little laugh, because I know Ms. Tremt doesn't mean a real trip. She meant reading a good book would take you on a trip in your imagination . . . didn't she?

Matt turns pale and looks at me like he wants

to run away as fast as he can. And that's just what he does. I couldn't understand his reaction. I mean, who doesn't love a good story, right? I couldn't wait to start reading this mysterious book.

CHAPTER	TITLE
2	Jump Off the Page

Ms. Tremt gets right down to business regarding *The Book of Memories*.

"Here's the deal, Jada," Ms. Tremt says. "If you like, you may bring two friends along to explore *The Book of Memories* with you. But they have to be there from the first turn of the page."

"I'll be right back," I reply, as I hand her back the book.

Daniel and Abby. Abby and Daniel. They're practically like one person to me they are such close friends.

Luckily, they're easy to find—they always hang around the broken vending machine after school to see if any extra snacks fall out. Well, Abby wants the extra snacks. Daniel's just along for the ride.

"Follow me," I whisper to them.

"Is this some fashion spy mission?" Daniel wonders.

"Close enough," I say. "We are needed in the library."

Abby groans. "Oh come on, Jada," she says. "I really don't want to study spelling words. Especially when there are gummy worms just waiting to drop."

Abby points.

I look at the vending machine and see that she is right. There is a package of gummy worms dangling from the machine's hook. I nudge the machine and the package falls. Then I reach in and grab the candy.

"Here, you can eat them later," I tell her. "Now let's go."

Okay, I will admit, that may have sounded a teensy bit bossy, but if you got a chance to hold

The Book of Memories, you would know it was necessary.

When we get back to the library, it's empty. Ms. Tremt must have sent everyone else home. She doesn't say a word to us, just leads us into that back room where she took Matt, Grace, and Luis earlier. Have I mentioned that Ms. Tremt has to use a fancy old-fashioned brass key to open the room up? Strange, no?

When we enter the room, we all gasp—even Ms. Tremt.

There's a Viking standing in the middle of the empty room.

"Where is my ship?" he bellows. "Why do I keep ending up back here?"

"Jada, Abby, Daniel, please give me a moment," Ms. Tremt says. We all nod, dumbfounded, and leave the room.

From behind the door we can hear the Viking yelling and Ms. Tremt saying something to him in a soothing voice. Then we hear some stomping and then a loud *thud*, like a book being slammed shut.

Ms. Tremt opens the door and leads us back

inside. She looks a bit shaken, but calm. And the Viking is gone!

"Where's the Viking?" Daniel asks.

"Back where he belongs," Ms. Tremt answers. Then she lets out a sigh.

"At least for now."

Abby, Daniel, and I exchange a look. But what can we do? Obviously Ms. Tremt doesn't want to discuss the mysterious Viking.

"All right, then. Where were we?" Ms. Tremt asks, holding up the ornate book.

"*The Book of Memories,*" Daniel reads aloud. "Whose memories are in there?"

"Excellent question," Ms. Tremt replies. "But I can't tell you the answer. You will have to find out for yourself."

Ms. Tremt hands the book back to me. I can't wait to open it, but I can only get to the title page. All of the other pages are stuck together. The only thing I see is an envelope and a due date card.

"How are we supposed to find an answer if we can't open the book?" Abby asks.

"Abby, this isn't just a book," Ms. Tremt

explains. "It is a portal to the past. It is full of the memories you choose to visit."

"Ms. Tremt, it isn't even April first." Daniel laughs. "And you can't fool us anyway."

"I'm not trying to fool anyone," Ms. Tremt says seriously. "And certainly not you three. You see, I have been given the honor of selecting a few lucky children to send on time-traveling adventures."

"By time-traveling adventures, you mean incredible stories where you get so lost in the book that you feel like you've literally traveled back in time," Daniel says. "Right, Ms. Tremt?"

"Wrong, Daniel," Ms. Tremt corrects him. "I mean literally taking a trip back in time."

"Matt, Grace, and Luis!" I gasp. "Is that what happened when they suddenly appeared in the library, like out of nowhere?"

"I can't reveal any information about my prior selections," Ms. Tremt says. "But I like the way you think, Jada."

The librarian continues. "I also like your creativity. And most of all, your huge, compassionate heart. I would like to offer you a time-traveling opportunity, Jada. You are free to accept or deny it, of course, along with your friends."

I open my mouth, but for once no words come out. I'm not sure exactly what I had expected when Ms. Tremt told me *The Book of Memories* would take me on a trip in "bold, new ways." But one thing is for sure. I know I definitely didn't think I'd be given a chance to travel back in time!

"Ms. Tremt, that sounds incredible," Abby chimes in. "But also pretty hard to believe, to be honest."

"Seriously, Ms. Tremt," Daniel adds. "Do you really expect us to believe that time travel is possible?"

My mind is racing as my friends talk to Ms. Tremt. I'm picturing that day a while back when a guy in an Albert Einstein costume walked over to Jeffrey Tyler in the library and tossed a book at him. I'm thinking of the clothes Matt, Grace, and Luis were just wearing, and how they just magically appeared with Ms. Tremt. I'm thinking of the Viking that just now mysteriously showed up and then disappeared. I'm thinking that it all makes sense if you believe in time travel. And if you don't, it all seems pretty crazy.

I look back at Ms. Tremt and see that the fountain pen in her hand is glowing.

"First I'm going to give you a glimpse of the infinite possibilities that await you," Ms. Tremt says. "Seeing is believing, as they say."

"And then?" Daniel asks.

"And then we will review the rules of time travel," Ms. Tremt says. "And you will pay close attention so you do not make any grievous errors during your journey. Because the fate of the future will be in your hands!"

Ms. Tremt uses the sparkling fountain pen to sign her name on the card in *The Book of Memories*. A question appears on the page. *Where would you like to go today?*

"Ooh, let's go back to when the Beatles first came to America!" Abby calls out.

"Let's see the building of the Great Wall of China!" Daniel says.

"How about the White House?" I suggest. "During Lincoln's time there. I'm working on a report about him and there's a fact I'd like to make sure is accurate."

"Abraham Lincoln, I like it," Ms. Tremt says. "He's a president I can take my hat off to."

"I can't remember ever seeing you wear a hat, Ms. Tremt," Daniel says.

"True, Daniel—a flip of the scarf, then." Ms. Tremt laughs.

May 20, 1962, White House, Washington, DC, Ms. Tremt carefully writes in the book with her beautiful fountain pen.

Then Ms. Tremt closes *The Book of Memories* and places it against the wall.

"Now stand back," she instructs us.

The book begins to shake.

And stretch.

And grow.

Higher and higher, wider and wider, until it fills the entire wall like a giant mural.

"Now you may open the book," Ms. Tremt declares.

I pull open the cover and instead of a blank page, an image of Lincoln's office fills the wall like a 3-D movie projection.

"Allow me to demonstrate quickly," Ms. Tremt says.

Ms. Tremt walks over to the wall and places her hand on—and then into—the scene. Her hand actually disappears into the wall and reappears inside the image. She waves it behind Abraham Lincoln's back.

Luckily, the president seems distracted and doesn't notice Ms. Tremt's hand at all. Instead, he takes off his tall black stovepipe hat and pulls out a pile of notes from it! Then he puts the hat back on his head and shuffles through the papers until he finds the one he wants.

"Awesome!" Daniel laughs. "Wow . . . so . . . Lincoln kept notes in that big hat. Who knew?"

"That's a way to make fashion work for you!" I laugh. "I just wanted to check that his face was really thin and that he had a beard."

"Really?" Daniel says. "Why?"

"I read that he grew it because an eleven-year-old girl wrote a letter to him when he was running for office," I explain. "She told him that his face was so thin it might scare off voters, so it would look a lot better if it were covered with whiskers."

"Wow," Abby says. "That's kind of mean."

"But she kind of had a point," I say. "I mean, check him out. He is rocking the whiskers."

Daniel walks over to the wall and touches it. His hand slips into the image and he jumps back in shock.

"SOOOO COOL!" he shouts. "And definitely *not* an illusion."

"Seeing is believing, as they say," Ms. Tremt says. "But better not to interfere with the leader of our nation at work. In fact, *The Book of Memories* insists that we do not interfere."

Then she closes the book and the scene disappears. We watch in awe as the book shrinks down to normal size.

"So is that kind of a time-travel rule?" Abby asks. "What about the rest of them? Are you going to fill us in on those now?"

"Of course," Ms. Tremt replies. "You are correct, Abby. The first rule, and the most important one is: You can't interfere with or change major events in history. You can't change the outcome of a battle, or warn people of a natural disaster about to occur, as much as you may want to."

"So no saving President Lincoln?" Daniel asks.

"Sad as it is, no saving President Lincoln, or anyone else," Ms. Tremt says. "You can make one small change that affects your life, or your family, in a positive way, but that's it. No saving-the-world type of changes."

As a "We Are the Change" type of person, I have to admit that news is a little disappointing, but understandable.

"You also can't act for purely selfish reasons," Ms. Tremt continues. "Time portals are powered by positive energy. And since time is elastic, positive energy is stronger than negative energy."

"Although some negative energy has been interfering with the time-travel continuum recently," Ms. Tremt says quietly. "But you don't have to worry about that; yours will just be a short trip."

"So where are we going?" Daniel asks.

"That's Jada's decision," Ms. Tremt explains. "She will have three hours of travel time from the second I write the date down in this book. It may seem a long time, but three hours will fly by, and when *The Book of Memories* starts to glow, you will have only ten minutes to return home or be stuck in the past forever.

"Jada, think of somewhere in time you'd like to spend three hours," she continues. "And I do mean think about it—you don't have to decide now. We'll talk more tomorrow."

Tomorrow sounds great, because right now I've got nothing. There are so many things I'd like to change in the world, but they're all big things, and Ms. Tremt said changing a major world event was off-limits.

We follow Ms. Tremt as she leaves the secret room.

"Of course, this is all confidential," she tells us. "No talking to anyone about it—including Matt, Grace, and Luis."

Ms. Tremt takes the key out of her pocket and locks *The Book of Memories* into her desk drawer. Then she flips her furry scarf and dives into a stack of books.

"Didn't your mom want to become a doctor?" Abby says as we walk to our lockers. "Maybe we should go back and help her."

"She did, but she also wanted to be an

astrophysicist, a genetic engineer, and a bunch of other things." I laugh. "She decided science teacher would be the perfect career because she'd get to study all those things. So she's all good, I think."

"What about your grandparents?" Daniel says. "Any way we can help them?"

"They're pretty happy too," I say. "I'll think more about it tonight. I'm sure we'll figure something out. But first I've got to figure out how to explain this bad grade on my spelling test to my mom."

"Yeah, good luck with that," Abby says.

"Thanks." I moan. "I need it."

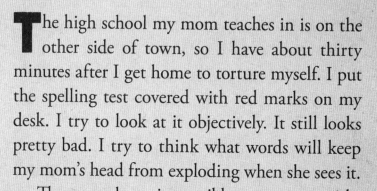

CHAPTER	TITLE
3	I Before E

The high school my mom teaches in is on the other side of town, so I have about thirty minutes after I get home to torture myself. I put the spelling test covered with red marks on my desk. I try to look at it objectively. It still looks pretty bad. I try to think what words will keep my mom's head from exploding when she sees it.

Those words are impossible to come up with.

Mom, I just read an article that said that too much importance is placed on correct spelling and grammar, I could argue.

I wouldn't be lying, either. I did read an article that said just that. It also said that English grammar doesn't actually work, and spelling mistakes can be a sign of creativity. And since I'm going to be a fashion designer, I think creativity is much more important than spelling.

I just know my mother will disagree. I'm right.

I hear the front door open and I decide to rip the bandage off quickly. I meet Mom in the kitchen with my spelling test and I hand it to her. I don't say a word, I just hang my head and peek up at her. She looks at it and shakes her head.

"This doesn't make me happy, Jada," she says.

"I know," I answer.

"You told me you studied," Mom adds, and I cringe at the idea that she might think I was lying.

"I did study, Mom," I say honestly. "It was like my mind went completely blank when I picked up my pencil. Like some ghost just wiped it clean with an eraser."

"That can't be easy, but we're going to have to figure out a way to fix it," Mom continues. "You do so much with your fashion designs and with your We Are the Change club. I'm sure you can do this, too. Remember, the more you learn, the more good you can do in the world."

"I know, Mom," I say. "I'll try."

Mom takes a pen, signs the paper, and hands it back to me. I go upstairs and shove it into my binder. I'd be happy if I never saw it—or another spelling word—again. I know my mom's wrong, anyway. Spelling some words correctly on a test might bring my average up, but I'm not going to need them when I'm working on dress designs, and they're definitely not going to change the world.

I have lots and lots of algebra homework, but I don't mind that at all. It takes my mind off the spelling words and Mom's face when she looked at my test. I will admit, though, that it is a little hard to focus on math when time-travel plans are waiting to be made.

I'm almost finished with my homework when I hear a knock on my door.

"Jada, come on. It's time to wash up for dinner," my little brother, Sam, calls. I get up and head down to the kitchen.

Sam is not bad as far as little brothers are concerned. I even like hanging out with him sometimes. But he has this annoying habit of always wanting to talk about the one thing I don't want to talk about.

"Hey, Jada, what were you and mom talking about before?" Sam asks as he passes me a bowl of broccoli. "You guys sounded so serious."

"We were talking about the importance of—" Mom starts, scowling.

"You know what I really want to talk about?" I interrupt. "Time travel! From a science teacher's perspective, of course. Do you think it's ever going to be possible, Mom?"

"Hmmm, interesting topic," Mom says. "I'm not sure what I think. I have read a bit about it, though, and there are some theories that make it seem plausible."

Perfect! I knew Mom couldn't resist a good science-related question.

"Einstein's theory of relativity, the famous 'energy is equal to mass multiplied by the speed of light squared' actually suggests time travel *is*

30

possible, at least in one direction," Dad chimes in. I smile to myself.

I prop my chin on my fist and stare intently at Mom and Dad as if I am completely absorbed in what they're saying, even though I understand only about a tenth of it.

"Yes!" Mom says, getting excited. "Einstein proposed that time and space are joined in our universe. They make up a four-dimensional fabric known as space-time. Time is an illusion—it's relative. Travel fast and time moves more slowly. So as a person in a spaceship approaches the speed of light, she would age much slower than her twin at home on Earth."

"Interesting," I say. It truly is, at least the parts I can wrap my brain around. I'm just more interested in keeping the conservation flowing so it doesn't return to spelling and studying. "But how does that mean time travel is possible?"

"Scientists have measured the movement of clocks at the top and bottom of skyscrapers. The clocks at the bottom ticked slightly slower than the ones at the top," Mom says.

"So the same principles that make those clock

hands tick slower should also work at extremes?" Dad asks.

"Exactly!" Mom cheers. "Some scientists even believe that past, present, and future might actually exist all at once, and we just aren't able to grasp how to travel through time yet because our perception is limited."

"Mom, can we just stay here?" Sam asks. "I like it here, and you're starting to make my head hurt. I'm happy with my friends, and my soccer team, and my video games. . . ."

"Of course, Sam," Mom says as she ruffles his hair. "We're not going anywhere, are we, Jada?"

"Huh?" I grunt, half listening to what Mom and Sam are talking about as I think about where I might be heading in *The Book of Memories*.

"I said we're not going anywhere," Mom repeats. "Sam's worried that we might hop into a time-traveling ship and leave him behind."

"A time-traveling ship?" I laugh. "No need to worry about *that,* Sam. I promise I will not be boarding any ships."

The best thing is, Sam would never even know that I left the present time. Ms. Tremt told us that even though we'd be gone for three hours, when we returned it would be like no time had passed. So I won't even have to text Mom and make up a story about having to stay late after school or anything. Because I wouldn't really feel good doing that.

I get up to help Dad clear the dirty dishes from the table, and we continue our discussion away from Sam. Dad is a copywriter in an advertising agency, so he loves discussing anything that makes you use your imagination. He tells me about the possibility of creating wormholes between points in space-time. And about cosmic strings, which are narrow tubes of energy stretched from one end of the universe to the other. I know, it's pretty mind-blowing, right?

"So if there were time-travel machines, they probably wouldn't look the way they're always pictured in movies and stuff, right?" I ask.

"Exactly," Dad says. "Some researchers think that time travel could begin in a doughnut-shaped vacuum that's surrounded by normal matter. Inside the doughnut, space-time could be bent."

"You know, you've gotten pretty smart

hanging around Mom all these years." I laugh.

"I know; it's crazy." Dad chuckles. "You should have seen some of my report cards when I was your age."

"Well, speaking of grades," I say. "There's something I need to talk to you about. . . ."

In the middle of the night, I wake up and my heart is pounding. Did you ever have that nightmare where you're paralyzed and you can't move or run or do anything but you need to escape or else? Well, I just did, and it seemed completely real. I was in the secret room behind the library, but I was completely alone except for some monstrous, humanoid letters and words. They held my hands and feet down so I couldn't move. A mysterious voice boomed out spelling rules over the intercom system.

"Rule one: *I* before *e*, except after *c* . . . ," the voice boomed.

"WHAT ABOUT 'WEIRD'?" I cried. "OR 'FEISTY' OR 'FOREIGN'?"

"Rule two: Add *s* or *es* to make a noun plural."

"CHILDREN! MICE! PEOPLE! TEETH!"
I screamed.

Then I woke up.

I rub the sleep out of my eyes and go to the bathroom to brush my teeth.

That's it, I think to myself. *I am done with spelling forever! When I grow up and make a lot of money as a top fashion designer, I'm just going to hire someone to spell all my words for me. I bet Aunt Katy doesn't worry about spelling—ever!*

Aunt Katy is my mom's big sister. Everyone says I got my fashion sense and creativity from her. She started off as a costume department intern at a movie studio in Hollywood, California. Now she's a buyer for a major department store (which means she picks the clothes that the store will sell), and she wears the most amazing outfits you've ever seen. I like Aunt Katy's style. I try to copy it a little myself.

When I get to school, Daniel and Abby are right where I would expect them to be, waiting by my locker.

"So, where are we going?" Abby asks. "Paris? Tokyo? The Big Bang?"

"Ooooh, I like that one," Daniel says. "Or how about the first moon landing?"

"Very interesting," I reply. "But that's not where we're going. I'm just not sure yet. As soon as I know, I'll tell you."

"Okay, but in case you need help, I did a little research last night," Daniel says.

Daniel hands me a rolled-up paper tied in a ribbon.

"I was going to text it to you, but I thought this looked a lot more time-traveler-y," he admits.

I untie the ribbon and the scroll unravels in my hand and rolls out onto the floor.

"That's quite a list," I say.

"Impressive, isn't it?" Daniel replies. "I did a quick Internet survey and asked, 'If you could witness one moment in history, what would it be?'"

"Daniel!" I yell. "Ms. Tremt told us to keep this confidential."

"I did!" Daniel yells back. "I didn't tell anyone we were going there. I just asked them where they would go. It's an anonymous poll too!

"And there were some great suggestions," he says.

Of course then he starts to recite them one by one because he has practically the whole list memorized.

"Gee, thanks," I say. "I'll look it over. And like I said, I'll let you know when I decide. Pinky promise."

During free period that day, I check out Daniel's list. I have to admit there are some interesting items. Da Vinci painting the *Mona Lisa*. The Beatles performing on a rooftop in London. Or for a patriotic trip, Betsy Ross sewing the first American flag.

My excitement dies in homeroom at the end of the day. As soon as I open my progress report, I can feel my insides turn over and over. My average has dropped so much because of that stupid spelling test.

"I know *exactly* where I want to go," I whisper to Abby, who is sitting next to me.

"Awesome! Where?" she asks.

"Back to last week," I tell her. "I'm going to retake that spelling test. One small change, right?"

"Right," Abby agrees. "Though not exactly

the most exciting time period in history . . ."

"I know," I say. "But if my Mom sees this progress report, she's going to freak."

"If you're sure that's what you want," Abby says, "I'm in."

"I knew you would be," I say. Then I sigh. "But now what am I going to tell Daniel?"

Daniel is reading through some texts on his cell phone when we meet up with him in the library. We're not allowed to use our phones during the day in school, but after dismissal it's allowed. Of course, as soon as the last bell rings, the hallways are full of kids tapping their cell phone screens furiously.

"I got a lot more suggestions, Jada," Daniel says excitedly when he finally realizes that Abby and I are standing right next to him.

"That's cool," I say. "But I've already figured

out where we're going. I hope you still want to go."

Daniel starts hopping from foot to foot.

"Do you need to use the bathroom?" I ask.

"No." Daniel laughs. "I just can't wait to hear this. I know you're going to pick the best place ever, and this is going to be the most exciting moment of my life!"

Abby starts to giggle.

"Think about it, Daniel. Isn't time travel—just the concept, on its own—exciting?" I ask. "It doesn't really matter where we go, right? It's the fact that we're going through time at all that's so cool."

"I guess so . . . ," Daniel says tentatively. "I'm a little afraid where you're heading, though, Jada."

"Okay, but what if I told you we were going back in time one week, so I could retake my spelling test? It would still be totally cool. To travel through time together. Right?"

"WHAT?" Daniel roars. "Could you pick a time even more boring than that, Jada? Let's see. . . . How about we go back to the moment this morning when I was flossing my teeth in the bathroom? Or better yet, when Abby was sitting at her kitchen counter, watching her mom make her tuna fish sandwich? Why not go there? That's pretty thrilling, don't you think?"

"It's my trip, Daniel," I say adamantly. "I get to choose. You get to come along, if you want. If you don't want to, fine."

"Aw, come on, Jada," Daniel whines. "You know I'll be there. But could you please give it a little more thought? I'm sure Ms. Tremt will let you have another day or two to figure it out. It's our one chance to time travel. Using it to go back and retake a test seems like such a waste."

"It will make my life so much better, though," I explain. "I can get my mom off my back for a while. She's been bugging me about spelling words almost every night. If she sees this progress report, I might be grounded for life."

"I think you're being a little dramatic," Daniel says. "But it is your trip."

"You know I'm ride or die, Jada." Abby laughs. "If that's where you want to go, I'll be there by your side. But I'm going to have to step onto Daniel's side for a minute."

"Okay," I say. "Let's hear it."

"IT'S A TIME MACHINE, JADA!" Abby yells. "Are you sure you want to use it to retake a spelling test?"

"I'm sure," I reply.

"It's a very logical choice," Ms. Tremt adds from nowhere.

Suddenly, she pops up from behind a desk. Her scarf looks shredded and she seems nervous. She keeps looking around as if she's expecting to see Dracula or some kind of scary monster appear in the library. For our sake, I hope not!

"I wouldn't expect any less from you, Jada," Ms. Tremt continues. "But I wonder if you would indulge me for a moment." Then she ducks down again.

Ms. Tremt looks from side to side and waves us over to her. Daniel, Abby, and I look from side to side, too, just to make sure Dracula isn't lurking behind a box of books. We crawl behind the desk with her.

"I'm afraid that I can't send you back to last week," Ms. Tremt whispers. "It would be unfair to the other students in your class."

"I don't understand," I say.

"I know," Ms. Tremt says. "But please trust me. I have a proposal I'd like you to consider for a moment."

"Okay," I reply.

"I wonder if you'd allow me to send you to 1977," Ms. Tremt suggests.

"YES!" Daniel cheers as he starts to hum the theme from *Star Wars*. "Yes! Yes! Yes! Yes! Yes! We can be one of the first to see Luke Skywalker and Darth Vader on the big screen! Now, that's worth taking a trip back in time!"

"Oooh, that's when my Aunt Katy worked in Hollywood," I say. "She was an intern in a movie studio then. I wonder if she knew anyone who worked on *Star Wars*. I bet she did. I never even thought to ask her."

"Well, now's your chance," Ms. Tremt says. "Because, if you'll agree to my proposal, that's exactly where you're going—to the movie studio where your Aunt Katy worked in Hollywood in 1977."

Abby and Daniel do a happy dance. I decide not to think about my progress report and join them. I mean, I can't let my best friends—or

Ms. Tremt—down, can I?

"We're going to Hollywood. . . . We're going to Hollywood," we sing together.

Then we pretend to pose like movie stars. Abby and I can do glam selfie poses like we were born to be on the silver screen. Daniel, not so much, but I think we'll all fit right in anyway.

"Unfortunately, your screen test will have to wait for the future," Ms. Tremt says. "The rules of time travel are strict. You must limit your conversations with anyone you encounter. You must not bring any items from the future back to the past—electronics, dated books, or money, things like that. Because if you show anything from the future while you're in the past, it will bounce you right back to the present. And under no circumstances can you tell your Aunt Katy who you are.

"Also, when you travel through time, you need to fit in as best you can," Ms. Tremt continues. "I have some clothes here to help with that. But in an emergency, a real emergency, you'll need one of these."

Ms. Tremt pulls open a large drawer in her

desk. It is full of the wacky, colorful scarves that she wears every day.

"Some fabric-of-time experts have been working on these for me," she says. "They've informed me that this batch of scarves is ready for a beta test."

"No way," Daniel says. "I am not wearing one of those."

"Hopefully you won't have to," Ms. Tremt says. "They *are* just in beta stage, which means there are probably a few kinks to work out."

"What kind of kinks?" I ask, a little worried.

"Nothing to worry your fashionable little head about." Ms. Tremt chuckles. "They really are just in case of emergency. The scarves are made of a special nano-fabric that you can compress into a small ball. They'll fit right in your pocket, along with *The Book of Memories*, Jada, which you will also need to keep on hand in its shrunken form."

"I can do that," I reply. "But what kind of emergency cases are we talking about?"

"Well, if you find yourself in a situation where you need to appear time-appropriate, but don't have the right outfit on hand, you can just wrap the scarf around yourself," Ms. Tremt explains. "You will see yourself as you are, but to other observers, it will appear that you are dressed appropriately for the times."

"A fashion lifesaver!" I cheer. "I can get on board with that!"

"Be careful, though," Ms. Tremt warns. "They haven't been tested beyond a fifteen-minute period, and in some tests the scarves have gotten rather glitchy well before that. And, whatever you do, do not take the scarves off in front of people. You will immediately return to the present—we think. We're not exactly sure about that."

"Great," Abby sighs sarcastically.

"The good news is, Daniel, that while you are in the past, no one will actually see you wearing the scarf," Ms. Tremt says. "Except your time-traveling companions, of course."

"Is that a pinky promise?" Daniel asks as he takes a scarf.

"Indeed it is," Ms. Tremt says.

Ms. Tremt takes our cell phones and hands us each a wristwatch, the ones where you actually have to be able to tell time from looking at the minute and hour hands. We hand her all the money we have, too, and Ms. Tremt gives us back bills that were issued before 1977, and a cheat sheet with some fast facts about 1977.

Jimmy Carter was president of the United States.

Laverne & Shirley *and* Happy Days *were the #1 TV shows.*

A loaf of bread cost less than fifty cents.

The Atari 2600 gaming system was released.

The first Apple II personal computers went on sale.

Popular musicians at the time were Rod Stewart, Fleetwood Mac, and the Bee Gees.

"Ms. Tremt, you're the expert," I say. "But how are a bunch of middle school kids going to explain what we're doing in a Hollywood studio? And what will I even say to Aunt Katy?"

"I've done my research, Jada," Ms. Tremt replies. "I always do. There's a Crane's Record Store a few blocks away from the studio. You can walk into the costume shop and pretend that you need directions to the record store. And I think you should pay a visit to the record store while you are there. You might find it . . . enlightening."

Daniel, Abby, and I stare at Ms. Tremt. Record store? What's that?

Ms. Tremt laughs and then quickly explains that records are vinyl disks that hold music information the way our electronic devices do now. Record stores sold those vinyl disks. They were also the place where all the cool kids hung out.

"Sounds like the place for us," Daniel says.

"Definitely," Abby agrees.

"Because we are so cool," I add. "Movie-star cool."

My favorite part of the trip preparation process is next—CLOTHES! Ms. Tremt pulls out a box of clothes from the secret back room. I can't wait to see what's inside. Then I see the polyester pants, ugly sweaters, and print tunics Ms. Tremt pulls out and realize that maybe I can wait. Some of the 1977 fashion items need to go back to the drawing board!

I'm able to pull together a decent outfit of wide-leg navy blue corduroys and a matching striped polo shirt for Daniel. Abby unfortunately gets lime green polyester slacks, which are pretty hideous, but I find a not-so-horrible smock top for her to wear with them. Then I dig deep and hit gold. At the bottom of the box is a cute orange minidress. Orange is not a color that looks good on everyone, but it does on me.

"Of course!" Abby complains. "You get the cute dress while I have to wear these horrible pants."

"Hey, it could be worse." I laugh. "But let me see what else I can find."

I rummage through the box some more. I know Abby likes to push the fashion envelope, so I find her some killer platform shoes and a cool sweater-vest.

"It's hobo chic," I tell her.

"Better," Abby says. "Not great, but definitely better."

"Jada, what was the name of the studio where your aunt worked?" Ms. Tremt asks.

"It started with a 'G,'" I say. "Galaxy . . . Galactic . . . Galaxian! That's it."

Ms. Tremt takes out her fountain pen and *The Book of Memories*.

"When I write your names in the book," she tells us, "the book will ask me where you would like to go. I will write down the exact place and year you would like to visit. You will immediately be transported to that time and place. When you see the ten-minute-warning glow, you will have exactly that amount of time to write the date you wish to return to, find a safe place to set the book down, and let it grow so that you may step back into the present day. Do *not* lose track of time. Now, please synchronize your watches. The time is exactly two thirty."

Ms. Tremt opens the book, takes the date card out of the envelope, and writes *Galaxian Studios, Los Angeles, California, June 1, 1977* with her fountain pen. Then she writes down all three of our names: *Jada Reese. Abby Morales. Daniel Chang.*

The book sparkles and the words *Where would you like to go today?* appear in glowing green text.

"Please make sure your watches are synchronized," Ms. Tremt says as the costume design studio appears on the wall.

As I check my watch, Ms. Tremt places a small pendant pin in my hand.

"Jada, I need you to trust me once more," Ms. Tremt says. "I can't explain the reasons at the moment, but I need you to place this pin with the jewelry in the costume studio and leave it there. Whatever happens, do *not* bring it back to the present."

"Got it, Ms. Tremt," I whisper back. "I trust you. And you can trust me too."

"I know." Ms. Tremt smiles.

I stand in the middle and hold Daniel's hand with my left hand and Abby's with my right. Suddenly a building with the name Galaxian Movie Studios appears in the book. My heart is pounding as I realize that we are actually going to travel through time and go to Aunt Katy's studio. But as we step in, the picture of the studio begins to fade.

"TIM RAVELTERE!" we can hear Ms. Tremt yell and gasp as we step into the scene. "Stay away from my kids!"

Once we're through the portal, things don't look like the studio at all.

"Uh-oh," Daniel gasps. "What's going on?"

Somehow, someway, we have not ended up in Hollywood, but by the banks of a river. Nearby, there's a woman with a baby on her back, gathering water and herbs from the river. Luckily, her back is turned to us. I remember Ms. Tremt told us if we wear her scarves, our clothes will change to whatever time period we are in.

"Scarves, now!" I command my friends. "We need to fit in."

We each take out the scarf from our back pockets, unfold it, wrap it around ourselves, and cross our fingers. To us, it just looks like we're dressed in wacky clothes and wearing even wackier scarves. Hopefully it looks totally different to her.

"Greetings, children," the woman says with a smile when she turns our way.

"Greetings," I reply, shell-shocked. "Who . . . uh . . . are you?"

"What year is this?" Daniel asks.

"Are you an actress?" Abby wonders.

"My name is Sacagawea," the woman says. "You don't know what year it is? It's 1805, and I am helping the explorers Lewis and Clark on their journey."

"I thought you looked familiar!" Abby gasps.

"I do?" Sacagawea says, confused. "Have we met before?"

"Um . . . no . . . not exactly," Abby stammers.

Then she pulls us into a huddle.

"Guys, remember what Ms. Tremt told us," Abby says. "*The Book of Memories* is so powerful, sometimes things can get a little wacky."

"But how is she speaking English?" Daniel asks, confused.

"It must be the scarves," I tell him. "They make everything understandable to us—and us to other people."

Abby turns back to Sacagawea.

"I think my cousin met you at the trading post," she bluffs.

"That may be so," Sacagawea replies. "Who is your cousin?"

"Hey, what are those herbs for?" Daniel interrupts, trying to change the topic. "Is someone sick? Is that a natural cure?"

Sacagawea laughs and holds her nose.

"It's a natural cure for . . . smelly body." She giggles. "Lewis and Clark are brave explorers, but it's been weeks since they've had a bath! I think that's why my baby cries whenever they're around!"

Daniel, Abby, and I laugh too. Those are definitely the things they *don't* tell you about in history class!

"This is amazing. Remind me to e-mail my teacher about Sacagawea when we get back," Abby says. "Oh wait. I forgot that I can remind myself with this."

Abby pulls out a thin pen that she got for her birthday and as soon as she does . . .

Boompf!

CHAPTER	TITLE
5	Ready, Set, Go

Abby is gone! Daniel and I are left standing with Sacagawea, who had luckily stopped to take care of her crying baby and had missed Abby's vanishing-into-thin-air act.

"Where did your friend go?" Sacagawea asks when she turns back to us.

"Oh, her, well, she forgot something back in the . . . ," Daniel begins.

"Back in our wagon," I finish.

"Well, I should get back to camp with these herbs," Sacagawea says. "It was nice to meet you."

"Same here," I reply. "See you around sometime."

We hurriedly wave to Sacagawea, and then Daniel and I are alone.

"Jada, what are we going to do?" Daniel moans. "Abby's gone and we don't know where she went, and we don't even know how to get out of here."

"I have an idea," I tell Daniel as I start to unwrap my scarf with one hand and take Daniel's hand in the other. "Hold on. I think if we hold hands we can get back together, but if not, just take off your scarf too."

As soon as I take off the scarf, since we are wearing clothes from 1977, we are immediately transported back to the present and the little room off the library. Abby and Ms. Tremt are both there, looking flustered.

"Oh, thank the time-space continuum!" Ms. Tremt sighs, obviously relieved to see us.

"What was that about?" I wonder. "Why didn't we go to 1977 as planned?"

"I'm not exactly sure," Ms. Tremt says, doing that thing where she looks nervously from side to side again. She looks a bit pale, too.

Daniel, Abby, and I look from side to side again too. It's like we can't help ourselves, the way you always have to yawn when you see someone else yawn.

"I have a confession to make," Abby says. "I might have been thinking about my Lewis and Clark report when we walked into the portal."

"Good! I mean, yes, yes, that must be it," Ms. Tremt says unconvincingly. "The portal must have picked up some time-wavelength vibrations."

"I *have* been eating, sleeping, and dreaming the explorer life this past week," Abby admits.

"And you got back because of . . . ?" Ms. Tremt asks curiously.

"This," Abby replies, holding out her pen.

"Ah, the ballpoint pen," Ms. Tremt says. "Definitely an anachronism in 1805."

"But wouldn't it have been fine in 1977?" Daniel asks, confused.

"Not really," Abby says. "I just realized why."

"Why?" I ask.

"Because this."

Abby presses a button on the pen to show

that it's not just a pen; it's a pen with a voice-activated recorder, and she'd just recorded the last five minutes of our conversation.

"Wow, pretty sneaky," I note. "I like."

"I'll take that," Ms. Tremt says. "I definitely don't want you taking it with you to 1977."

"And you two?" Ms. Tremt asks as she turns to me and Daniel. "How did you get back here?"

"Scarf removal," I say.

"Good thinking," Ms. Tremt says

Ms. Tremt uses Abby's pen to scribble a note on a yellow pad. Surprisingly, the note doesn't mention anything about 1805, or Lewis and Clark, or even history fair. It just has two names on it with an arrow connecting them. Tim Raveltere and Abby Morales. *Who is Tim Raveltere?* I wonder.

"Are you willing to try this again?" Ms. Tremt asks. "I can understand if you'd like to refuse the offer, considering what just happened."

"But that was my fault," Abby says.

"Oh yes, right." Ms. Tremt laughs nervously. "Are you sure you can clear your mind of history?"

"I'm sure," Abby says.

"Ms. Tremt, can we go already?" Daniel laughs. "I am so ready to get to 1977."

Ms. Tremt turns to me and gestures to my pocket.

"I still have it, Ms. Tremt," I whisper as I touch the pendant in my pocket. "No worries."

Ms. Tremt tells us to focus on the year 1977 and to keep it in our minds. She signs the card in *The Book of Memories* again and underlines the year "1977" three times for emphasis.

"It is now 2:45 p.m.," Ms. Tremt says. "You must return to the present by 5:45 p.m., or risk being stuck in 1977 forever. Do not lose track of time! And stay together!"

"We will, Ms. Tremt!" we all say.

"Tim Raveltere. Tim Raveltere. Tim Raveltere," Ms. Tremt whispers as the book starts to glow. "You may have found me after all these years, but you have met your match . . . and more."

"What's that?" I ask.

"Never mind," Ms. Tremt says. "I didn't realize I was talking aloud."

I post the name Tim Raveltere in my brain like a sticky note on my bulletin board at home.

There's something more to this than Ms. Tremt is telling us, but I'll have to figure that out later. First things first, and right now 1977 is the first thing on my list.

The Book of Memories glows and grows. Once again the costume shop at Galaxian Movie Studios appears on the wall in front of us. I imagine what it will be like to see Aunt Katy the way she looked back then. I close my eyes and take a deep breath; then I grab Daniel's and Abby's hands again.

"Ready?" I say.

"Set," Abby says.

"Go!" Daniel shouts.

CHAPTER	TITLE
6	The Studio
	2:46 p.m. (2 hours, 59 minutes left)

We land right in front of the door to the costume shop. When we open the door and step in, the very first person I see is Aunt Katy. It must be her; she has the same exact smile as my cousin Daja, the way her lips curl without opening and her whole face scrunches up with happiness. It's so unsettling to see her so young I literally stop breathing for a second.

People have always said that Daja is a clone of her mom, and I can see that they look a lot alike, but now that Aunt Katy is here; young and standing across the room from me, it's pretty spooky.

It's also pretty spooky, and amazing, to see that Aunt Katy is a total teenage diva! The bell-bottoms at the end of her jeans are so wide they look like elephant legs. Her platform sandals lift her at least six inches off the ground and are bloodred with pink, yellow, and orange stripes. They match the color in the petals of the flower that is stuck in the front of her gigantic Afro. She looks so funky she makes me want to dance!

"Hey, sunshine. Need help?" Aunt Katy shouts from behind her sewing machine.

I am a deer. And I am completely caught in the headlights. My mouth tries to form words, but no sounds come out.

Come on, people, it's my Aunt Katy! This funkadelic fashion teen changed my diapers once upon a time! Give me some room to be shell-shocked with awe.

"Um, hey there," Abby says. "We're looking for Crane's Record Store."

Thank you, thank you, thank you, Abby!

"We were just hoping someone could help

us with the directions," Daniel adds.

"Groovy record store," Aunt Katy comments. "I can tell you how to get there if you make me a promise."

"Okay," Daniel says. "What is it?"

"Promise you're not going to buy that new Billy Joel album." Aunt Katy groans. "I'm so sick of him. He's just a flash in the pan. And I'm tired of hearing him sing, 'Say goodbye to Hollywood.' You know what, Billy? Say hello to Hollywood! It's a pretty happening place."

"Wow, why don't you tell us how you really feel about him?" Abby laughs.

Aunt Katy opens her mouth and lets out an enormous laugh.

"You're funny," she tells Abby. "But mark my words, people are going to get tired of him soon."

I try hard not to giggle. Aunt Katy knows fashion, that's for sure, but I'm not so sure her musical predictions are on point, considering that Billy Joel is still selling out stadiums.

"You know you stumbled into a costume shop, right?" Aunt Katy laughs as she sees me staring at all the racks of clothes.

"Yeah, it's kind of hard to miss that," I say, finally finding some words.

"Well, most kids don't get a chance like this every day," Aunt Katy says. "Want to try on some costumes?"

Abby and I cheer. Daniel waves his hand as if to say, *I'm good*.

"Come on, Daniel," Abby says as she drags him over to a rack filled with Victorian-era ball gowns and fancy men's suits. "Like she said, we don't get a chance to dress like this every day!"

Abby hands Daniel a top hat and a fancy long coat. I pull a red taffeta ball gown out and sigh. The bustle in the back is a thing of beauty.

"Put it on," Aunt Katy says. "You know you want to."

I do. I really do. And let me tell you, when it's on me, it looks ahhhMAZING! The skirt is full and I twirl around in it happily. I feel like a princess.

Abby tries on a dress that's even frillier, with endless ruffles and bows. It's totally not her style, but she's rocking it.

"Can we move on now?" Daniel groans.

"Sure," Aunt Katy says. "How about a little sci-fi?"

Aunt Katy pulls out a trunk filled with space-crew gear and alien masks.

"Now we're talking!" Daniel says as he slips into a goofy Martian mask.

"Do you find me repulsive?" he growls in what I guess he thinks is a Martian voice.

"Totally!" Abby and I laugh.

Aunt Katy leads us around the studio, and we try on superhero capes, princess tiaras, and evil-villain cloaks. It's better than the dress-up center we had in preschool!

While we're trying on clothes, I get to talk to Aunt Katy some more. I don't give her any information that will mess with the space-time continuum. I just want to know more about her, and it's a lot easier to talk to teenage Aunt Katy than the busy career woman who is always running around in the present.

"Did you always want to be a costume designer?" I ask.

"No. I got lucky," Aunt Katy says. "My art teacher last year saw some of my drawings, and she recommended me to one of her friends who works at Galaxian's costume shop. She runs the internship program here.

"I was a little nervous about interning for such an important studio, especially because I'm still in high school," Aunt Katy continues. "But I applied for it anyway, and I got it!"

"So someday you're going to run this place?" I laugh.

"That's not really my dream," Aunt Katy admits.

"What is?" I ask.

"I want to open my own boutique," Aunt Katy explains. "Working on costumes is a lot fun, and it's amazing to see them up on the big screen. But it's pretty stressful, too. Deadlines, budgets, they can drive you nuts. When it's crunch time, it's *crunch* time. Everyone here is so stressed out. My dream is to make some interesting clothes that real women can wear and sell them at my own shop. You know, for girls who look like me and you, and not just actresses."

"That sounds like a cool dream," I say. I don't tell her that her dream doesn't come true,

66

because the Aunt Katy I know doesn't have her own boutique or her own clothing line. She buys clothes from other designers to sell at the store.

"Owning a boutique is a great dream if you have a lot of money." Aunt Katy laughs. "For now I'm just paying attention, studying hard, and keeping my dream alive."

I turn around to find Daniel and Abby. She's wearing a cowboy hat and holding a lasso, and Daniel's dressed like the front end of a steer. I can't even.

"Have you worked with any celebrities?" I ask. "Have you made costumes for movie stars?"

"Well, not me, exactly," Aunt Katy says. "But they have to make sure the costumes fit perfectly, and that means measuring them. So I've been around when Paul Newman, Sally Field, and Sidney Poitier were here."

I make a mental note to learn more about these celebrities when I get home.

I know we're going to have to leave soon, but I could stay here all day. Then I put my hand in my pocket and suddenly remember my secret mission—the pendant Ms. Tremt gave me.

"Do you have any jewelry here?" I ask Aunt Katy.

"Are you kidding?" Aunt Katy says. "Check this out!"

Aunt Katy leads me to an enormous trunk full of jewelry . . . gold, beads, earrings, rings, bracelets. You name the jewelry, it's in there.

"Have fun," Aunt Katy says. "I have to get back to work. When you're ready, just let me know and I'll tell you how to get to Crane's."

When Aunt Katy's back is turned, I slip my hand into my pocket, grab the pendant, and drop it into the trunk.

"What are you doing?" Abby hisses from behind me.

"What are *you* doing?" I ask. "Spying on me?"

"Jada, we're not supposed to bring things from the future here, remember?" Abby reminds me. "Ms. Tremt warned us not to."

"I remember," I tell her. "But Ms. Tremt gave me this pendant and asked me to leave it here, so I figure I'd better follow her orders."

"That's weird," Abby says. "Didn't she wear it to school the other day? I remember because I told her how much I liked her new pendant and she said it had just popped up in a store she was in and she couldn't resist buying it."

"She absolutely asked me to leave it here," I say. "So that's what I'm doing."

Daniel walks over to us.

"What are you talking about?" he asks.

"Ms. Tremt asked Jada to leave a pendant here in 1977," Abby says.

"Pendant?" Daniel says. "The one she just started wearing recently? The one she wore for the first time three days ago with a red and yellow fuzzy scarf with her black dress with gold buttons down the back?"

I know what you're thinking. What's up with Daniel? Is he obsessed with Ms. Tremt? No, it's just that he has the most amazing photographic memory. He looks at something—or someone—once and remembers everything about their appearance forever. I had heard the expression "photographic memory" before, but I never met someone who truly had one before Daniel.

"Yes, that's the pendant," I say. "Anyway, I left it in the shop. Mission accomplished."

"Good. We'd better go now," he says. "It looks like Aunt Katy is super busy."

We look over and Aunt Katy has a pencil in her mouth, a pad in one hand, and a tape measure in the other. She's taking orders from one of the other workers in the shop.

Abby and Daniel step up to say good-bye to Aunt Katy. They're pushed out of the way when a coworker squeezes between them and hands Aunt Katy a piece of paper.

"Sorry," the coworker says. "But this is urgent."

Aunt Katy stares at the numbers on the paper and frowns.

"Remember when Edna dictated that list to you," the worker says, "and I asked you to send in the order? Check it out."

"What happened, Alex?" she grumbles. "These numbers are way over Edna's budget!"

"I don't know," Alex answers. "But some heads are going to roll, that's for sure."

"Yeah, my head," Aunt Katy says.

"Are you okay?" I ask Aunt Katy.

"Not really, but it's a grown-up problem,"

Aunt Katy replies. "And I'm not even a grown-up!" She laughs. "I'm still a teenager—I'm too young to be dealing with problems like this. But it's nothing for you to worry about. It's money stuff. Grown-up stuff is always money stuff. Remember that."

"Well, I want to work in fashion someday too," I tell her. "I'd like to learn what kind of grown-up problems I might have to deal with."

Aunt Katy shows me the paper. There are lines for different types of fabric, with numbers for each type.

"It's a fabric estimate," Aunt Katy explains. "For a dozen ball gowns for a new movie."

I look over the paper. I have no way of knowing if the prices are accurate, but I quickly add them up and they're correct.

"The numbers add up," I say. "So I don't know how they can be wrong."

"That was fast," Aunt Katy says, impressed. "Are you some kind of math whiz?"

"Something like that." I laugh. "You know, I don't know much about fabric prices, but it doesn't seem surprising to me. Silk satin is really expensive. Maybe that's why the total is so high?"

Aunt Katy grabs the paper from me and puts her finger on the line that says "silk satin."

"Silk satin?" she says. "Edna asked for pricing for sateen. It's a lot cheaper."

She fumbles around in her desk drawer and grabs a sheet of paper.

"See?" she says when she hands the paper to me. "This is a copy of my original order request."

"What's sateen?" Abby chimes in. "I'm fashion clueless."

"It's just a type of fabric," I explain. "It's silky, but it's made of cotton so it's cheaper than regular satin. It just has a satin gloss."

I point to Aunt Katy's paper.

"This might be the problem," I say.

Then I point to the word "SATEN."

"It's actually spelled S-A-T-E-E-N," I say. "Someone must have thought you just misspelled *satin* and ordered that."

"You're a genius!" Aunt Katy cheers and gives me a hug.

"A spelling genius," Daniel jokes.

"Hardly," I say. "I've just been trying hard

to make notes of the words I read. And most of what I read is related to fashion."

"You must have a big pile of notes, then," Aunt Katy says.

"Oh, they're not real notes," I explain. "I just try to remember to stick them to my brain."

"Well, however it works, thank you!" Aunt Katy says. "You're a lifesaver! I could have totally lost my internship over this!"

"Wow, that would have been awful for you," Daniel says.

"You have no idea," Aunt Katy adds. "This is a small industry. If you get fired from one studio, even if you're just an intern, you're probably not going to get hired anywhere else."

Aunt Katy grabs the telephone—one of those old-fashioned phones with a windy cord and push buttons—and gets the pricing for sateen. She crosses out the number on the estimate, and I add up the numbers quickly.

"Crisis avoided." Aunt Katy sighs.

Just in time, because Aunt Katy's boss waltzes into the studio.

"What's this?" she barks, pointing at Abby.

"I hope this is not one of our costumes."

Abby gasps and freezes in place, still in the cowgirl outfit.

"N-n-no, no, no, Edna," Aunt Katy stammers. "These kids are just here for some fittings. Those are their own clothes."

"Tragic," Edna huffs.

Aunt Katy may look like a fashion diva, but Edna has the diva attitude down pat. She flips through papers, criticizes stitches, and sends bolts of fabric flying across the room.

Workers scurry around like buzzing bees, moving this way and that at her every command. It's pretty impressive. I can see why Aunt Katy was so afraid to make a mistake.

"Do you have that ball gown estimate?" Edna barks at Katy.

Aunt Katy hands it to her. I can see her fingers cross behind her back.

"Hmm . . . okay . . . not bad . . ." Edna's fingers scan each line of the budget. "Good work here, Kathy."

"It's Katy," Aunt Katy says quietly.

"Right," Edna says.

Then she leaves the room in a whirlwind. I see one woman start to cry a little bit at her sewing machine. It's that intense.

"She hardly ever talks to me!" Aunt Katy squeals. "Especially not to say something nice. You're my lucky charm!"

"We'd better get going," I say to her. "You look like you have better things to do than let a bunch of kids hang around the studio."

"Nah, it's cool." Aunt Katy walks us over to the door and points down the street.

"Go straight for two streets, then make a right," she says. "Crane's is down the block on the left." Then Aunt Katy looks at me and smiles.

"I like you, kid," Aunt Katy says. "There's something about you . . . I can't quite put my finger on it, but it's something I like."

"Thanks for letting us look around," I say appreciatively. "I'll never forget it."

"You're a great kid," Aunt Katy tells me.

I give Aunt Katy an extra-squeeze-y hug, figuring that hugs can sometimes say things that words can't. I try to let my hug show how very much it meant to meet her, in this time, in this place, even if I'm not allowed to actually say it.

Before I can finish thanking Aunt Katy, a strange man bursts in on our conversation. He has dark hair and darker eyes and his expression looks worried, and a little devious, too. He's wearing a long leather coat, even though we're in Hollywood and it's eighty degrees out! Sweat is pouring from his forehead.

"Excuse me," he says to Aunt Katy. "I'm looking for a woman. She's about forty, serious gray eyes, and she has a proclivity for wacky colorful scarves."

My inner warning bell starts to ding. This guy is describing Ms. Tremt to a T.

"That sounds an awful lot like . . . ," Daniel starts to say cluelessly.

I decide a coughing fit is appropriate at the moment. Everyone looks at me, concerned, but I wave them off.

"Haven't seen her around here," Aunt Katy says. "Have you tried one of the sets? There are always new people buzzing around them."

The guy taps his wristwatch repeatedly and furrows his eyebrows.

"I'm positive she's around here," the guy adds nervously. "*Right* here."

"Well, she's not," Aunt Katy says, starting to sound stern.

"We didn't see anyone like that here," I add firmly.

Then I have a thought.

"What did you say your name was anyway?" I ask, knowing he never said his name. "If we see someone who looks like that, we'll let her know you're looking for her."

"No need for that, kid," the guy says. "Sorry to waste your time. Have a nice day."

The guy scurries away as quickly as he came.

"I don't trust that guy," Aunt Katy says, watching him leave. "Be careful, okay?"

"We will," I assure her. "I have a feeling he's going to stick around here for a while anyway, and we're heading in the opposite direction."

"Okay, well, catch you on the flip side," Aunt Katy says.

"Right, catch you on the, um, flip side," Abby says awkwardly.

When Aunt Katy closes the door, we all look

at one another and shrug our shoulders.

"Flip side." Daniel laughs. "What's that about?"

"I have no idea," I answer.

I do have an idea about the guy we just met, though. I'm just not ready to tell Daniel and Abby yet. I know because I saw the initials "TR" stamped on his briefcase.

"Tim Raveltere," I whisper to myself. "And so we meet."

That was weird," Daniel says as he shakes his head. "Didn't it sound like that guy was describing Ms. Tremt?"

"He was," I reply. "I think it has something to do with the pendant."

"The one you left with the other jewelry?" Abby asks. "I knew there was something going on with it!"

She gives me a little punch on the arm, as if to say, "Why didn't you tell me?"

I fill Abby and Daniel in on the details. I tell

them I have no idea why Ms. Tremt wanted me to leave the pendant in 1977, just that she did. I also tell them about the initials "TR" and the name Ms. Tremt wrote on her pad and said aloud before we walked into the portal.

"Do you really think he's looking for Ms. Tremt?" Abby asks.

"I do," I admit. "I don't know what he wants, but I don't think it's good."

"So that's the small change, then?" Abby wonders. "That's why Ms. Tremt asked you to come here instead of going back to the spelling test? So you could drop the pendant."

"I guess so," I say. "I mean, I did get to help Aunt Katy out, but I don't think that's a big deal really."

"Well, there's not really anything we can do about that mysterious guy," Daniel says. "I mean, Ms. Tremt isn't here, so she has nothing to worry about. Right?"

"Right," Abby agrees. "We should just head to the record shop while we still have time."

"I don't know, guys." I sigh. "I think we should follow Tim Raveltere—if that is Tim

Raveltere—and see what he's up to. He's super shady."

"Even if I thought that was a good idea," Abby starts, "what are we going to tell people when they ask us why we're walking around a movie studio?"

"We could be kid actors," Daniel suggests. "That's what Katy told Edna, remember?"

"Great idea!" I say. "If anyone asks, we're just kid actors who wandered away from the set of the movie."

"What movie?" Abby wonders. "You know someone's going to ask."

"I don't know, but we can always say they haven't decided on a title for it yet," I reply. "Since we're not supposed to really interact with anyone, let's try to keep on the down low."

"'Time Spies!'" Daniel says. "I like the sound of that!"

Abby and I agree that it does sound pretty sweet. We look around for a spot where we can lie low until Tim Raveltere comes back. I know he's coming back. It's the pendant, I'm sure of it, and I know he'll be back to find it.

We see a couple of workers building a set close to the costume studio and we decide to stick around there for a bit. You know how my mom was saying that Einstein said time is relative? I believe it. If I were standing around waiting for someone back home, I know it would have felt like an eternity. But watching all the crazy characters walking around Galaxian Studios? Time just flies!

First some animal trainers lead a group of camels right past us. Then a squad of actors dressed like Civil War soldiers march by, followed by the biggest pumpkin coach I have ever seen— to be honest, the only pumpkin coach I had ever seen in real life.

"That must be for a Cinderella movie!" Abby gushes.

"You think?" I laugh. "It's definitely not for *Night of the Living Gourds.*"

It's a good thing we're watching the coach closely, though, because otherwise we would have missed Tim Raveltere, dressed as Prince Charming, tiptoe out of the coach and into Aunt Katy's fashion studio.

He comes out five minutes later holding something shiny in his hand.

"Ms. Tremt's pendant!" I gasp.

If Tim Raveltere has a plan for what to do with the pendant, we couldn't figure it out from his actions. He actually looks pretty lost and confused. He keeps looking at the pendant, and his watch, and tapping them.

The gears in my logical brain are starting to grind. I'm thinking the pendant must be some kind of tracking device. As Abby mentioned, the pendant was pretty new. Ms. Tremt just got the pendant and suddenly she was acting all "who's hiding around the corner" and stuff. Weird things were happening with *The Book of Memories*. And she sent us here, to 1977, even though the time period was supposed to be my choice.

Clearly Tim Raveltere thought Ms. Tremt would be here, in 1977 Hollywood, at Galaxian Studios—not just her jewelry. He was looking for *her*.

"Ms. Tremt definitely wanted to get rid of the pendant," I say to Abby and Daniel. "I think she discovered that the pendant was actually a way for Tim Raveltere to track her down. I don't know why she's hiding from him, but I'm pretty convinced that she is."

We watch as Tim checks the pendant a few more times and then begins to sneak around the studio. He prowls around an old Western town, so we do, too. The funny thing is that most of the buildings aren't buildings at all, just a flat front that is propped up by some poles. Then Tim goes into a building, so we go in too. It looks like an empty hospital, but again, a lot of the props are, well, props. They're made of cardboard and tape and aren't at all like the real thing when you look at them up close. We visit a few city scenes—Paris, New York, and Chicago. Best of all, caterers are busy setting up a catering table in Chicago. Since they think we're actors, they offer us some freshly baked cookies. We don't want to blow our cover, so we're forced to eat them. It was rough, ha-ha.

Even rougher, though, is that while we're hanging around Chicago eating cookies, the director shows up and tries to put us to work.

"You're the extras, right?" he shouts at us.

"What are you waiting for? We've been looking for you!"

Daniel, Abby, and I pretend to follow him, but as soon as we can, we jump into a golf cart and duck. In a few minutes the director is out of sight, but so is Tim Raveltere.

"What are we going to do now?" Daniel asks. "This place is huge. He could be anywhere by now. I wouldn't know where to start."

"You're right," I admit. "But there must be a clue somewhere."

"You know, Ms. Tremt did tell us to go to Crane's," Abby says. "Maybe that *is* a clue. There has to be a reason she wants us there."

It sounds logical to me. So that's where we head.

CHAPTER	TITLE
8	Time Wars
	4:15 p.m. (1 hour, 30 minutes left)

Now comes the part where Daniel loses his mind, and his cool, if he ever had any. It turns out there's a movie theater right across the street from Crane's. The marquee shows the movie title in gigantic letters. It's funny too, because there's only one movie playing at this theater, not six like the theater back home.

Daniel starts to point at the marquee and jump up and down. He's making noises that don't actually sound human. They would fit right into a movie about life on alien planets, though.

"Daniel, are you okay?" Abby asks.

"EEP-AACK-ZORK-GLOBBADA!" Daniel replies.

I grab Daniel by the shoulders and shake him.

"Get ahold of yourself, Daniel!" I yell. "It's just a movie."

Daniel starts to shake and breathe heavily. I wouldn't be surprised if next his shirt rips open and he transforms into some hulking green monster. I mean, if time travel is possible, why not? He gives me a withering look.

"Just . . . a . . . movie?" Daniel hiss-whispers. "Just . . . a . . . movie?

"JUST A MOVIE?" he shouts. "Jada, you're my best friend, but you have no idea what you're talking about. *Star Wars* is not just a movie. *Star Wars* is an epic work of art. It's life changing. It takes you out of this world and into another universe. As soon as the words 'A long time ago in a galaxy far, far away,' appear on-screen, you are taken away—away from homework and chores and spelling tests and straight into the greatest, most thrilling battle between the forces of good and evil. Trust me, the feelings you get watching this movie are not like any other feelings you've ever had. It is one-of-a-kind experience."

"Um, does that mean that you like it?" Abby laughs.

Daniel gives her a friendly shove.

"If we just had a few more hours!" Daniel cries. "I could see it here—in one of the original showings in 1977. These people had no idea how epic the movie they were about to see actually was!"

I point to the guy dressed up in the Darth Vader outfit waiting in line to buy a ticket.

"I think you might be wrong about that, Daniel." I laugh.

I don't share Daniel's love for the movie, but I do love my friend, and my heart hurts a little for him. I wish we had enough time to watch the movie with Daniel. But my logical brain knows we don't, so Abby and I shove him through the doors of Crane's Record Store.

It feels like we *have* traveled to a whole new universe when we step inside the store. I've never seen anything like it in the present, but it is obviously a very popular place in 1977.

Records. Vinyl. LP. It's not like I'm totally

clueless. I kind of know what a record is, and I think my grandmother might still have some in her attic. Here's the down low: Once upon a time, before you could buy a song with a click of your touch pad, music was stored on flat black vinyl disks, about the size of a Frisbee. The disks were stored in square cardboard folders called album covers, which could look pretty wild and artistic.

Every inch of Crane's is filled with records. Most are stored in bins so you can flip through them easily. The store is organized so it's easy to find what you want. The rows of bins are labeled according to the musical genre, and in each genre the records of the musical artists are in alphabetical order. There are other albums on display, new releases that are being promoted, "manager's specials," and the most popular records.

But it seems like Crane's experience is more than just "run into the store, grab the record you want, and pay for it." It is definitely a place for music lovers to hang out. The salespeople all look young and cool, and they are *really* into their jobs. We watch them talking to customers, asking about their musical tastes and making suggestions.

"Dude, you have to check out The Clash," a guy with a ripped-up T-shirt tells one customer. "Your mind will be blown. Promise."

The customers in the store are as interesting as the album covers. There are punk rockers with studded leather belts. Glam rockers with sparkly makeup and shiny clothes. Disco queens in high heels and sequins. Funky fashionistas who look like they might have raided Aunt Katy's closet.

Abby and Daniel agree that Crane's is awesome. We linger in the rows of records. Music blares in every nook and cranny of the store. When a new song starts with the sound of chimes and some "wooo oooh ooohs," the salesclerks jump into a line and shout, "Do the Hustle!"

Some of the customers follow the order and line up in the rows of the store. Abby, Daniel, and I stand and stare with our mouths open as we watch them roll their hands and step forward and back, then side to side. Everyone seems to know just what to do!

"Come on!" a girl with big rose-colored glasses calls to us. "Do the Hustle!"

"Um, what's that?" I ask.

"Have you been living in a cave?" The girl laughs.

"No, we go to a really tough school, so we have to study all the time," Abby bluffs. "We don't get out much."

"Unbelievable!" the girl says, as she points to the guy with the ripped T-shirt. "Even Steve knows the Hustle. Although he'd probably drink sour milk before he was caught dead doing it."

The girl, whose name is Rosa, tells us to follow her moves. Four steps back, then clap. Four steps forward, clap. Then a series of moves called the "Rolling Grapevine," "Eggbeater," and "The Chicken." I'm going to leave those to your imagination.

While I'm in the middle of doing an Eggbeater, who should walk into the store but my Aunt Katy.

"Hi!" I call to her while still dancing. "What are you doing here?"

"I'm just meeting my mom here before we go

to lunch," Aunt Katy says. "And here she is."

When Aunt Katy says her mom, it takes me a minute to realize she's talking about my grandmother. Gran doesn't look like the person who makes me mac and cheese and washes my clothes for me, though. She's superfly!

Gran looks so cool it's hard not to stare. Flowery crop top, denim miniskirt, and the most fantastic pair of silver knee-high boots. I'm going to have to make a trip up to her attic when I get back to see if she still has those stashed away somewhere.

"This is my mom, Brenda," Aunt Katy says. "She doesn't get out much anymore with my little sister at home, but my sister's at a friend's house today." Katy turns to her mother. "Looking good, Mom." She laughs. "Much better than that housedress you've been wearing all day every day."

"Well, there's only room for one diva in a family," Brenda says. "And you're our diva, Katy."

"It's nice to meet you," Daniel and Abby interrupt, both of their eyes open as wide as they can get. They know my gran, and I can tell from their expressions they're in shock too.

"So you guys danced to the Hustle?" Brenda says. "What other kinds of music do you like?"

"Um—not Billy Joel?" Abby says, remembering Aunt Katy's warning.

Both Aunt Katy and Gran crack up.

"How about soul?" Brenda asks. "Funk?"

"We study a lot," Daniel says. "We don't know a lot about music."

Brenda calls Rosa over. I can tell that they're friends, and Rosa is happy to cater to her requests.

"We need to give these kids a quick lesson," Brenda tells Rosa. "Can you play a few songs for me?"

"Sure," Rosa says. "What am I playing?"

"'Shining Star' by Earth, Wind, and Fire," Brenda says. "And then 'Don't Leave Me This Way' by Thelma Houston."

"Got it," Rosa says.

It's impossible not to dance to the beats of the songs. The whole store turns to watch as Aunt Katy and Gran show off their moves. The last time I saw them dance was at my cousin George's wedding, and they definitely didn't move like that! They are amazing.

"I was on *Soul Train* last year," Aunt Katy tells us with a proud grin.

We have no idea what she's talking about, and it obviously shows.

"These kids are a little clueless." Rosa laughs. "*Soul Train.* It's a musical television show where they play the latest tunes and everyone dances."

"Got it," Abby says. "Sounds . . . funky."

We all laugh at the way Abby says "funky."

I would really like to hang out with 1977 Gran and Aunt Katy until the end of our time here, but I know time is running out and we still need to search the record store for clues. I say good-bye to Gran and Aunt Katy.

"It was nice to meet you," Gran says to me.

"Nice to meet you, too," I reply. "Thanks for the music lesson."

Aunt Katy leans in to give me a hug.

"Thanks again for saving my back," she whispers.

"It was nothing," I whisper back.

Once Aunt Katy and Gran are gone, it is back to the task at hand.

"This record store is amazing," Abby says,

"but I don't see any clues about Tim Raveltere. Where would we even start to look?"

I pull Ms. Tremt's cheat sheet from my pocket. I remembered she mentioned some of the most popular music from 1977.

"Ms. Tremt's sheet mentions Rod Stewart, Fleetwood Mac, and the Bee Gees," I say. "So let's start in those sections."

Abby heads off to find Rod Stewart, I take Fleetwood Mac, and Daniel takes the Bee Gees. It takes only a few seconds before Daniel starts waving a piece of paper and calling to us.

"It's a clue," Daniel says. "Actually, more like a warning."

I take the paper from him.

> *Do not let Tim Raveltere get ahold of*
> The Book of Memories
>
> *UNDER ANY CIRCUMSTANCES!*

I pat my back pocket just to make sure the book is still there, and I breathe a sigh of relief. It is. And Tim Raveltere is nowhere in sight.

"But what about the pendant?" Abby says. "Ms. Tremt doesn't mention it at all. So I guess our work is done here. We should probably head back home now."

"Probably," I say. "But let's just look around for five more minutes, okay?" I turn and look around. "Where's Daniel?" I ask.

Daniel has already run out of the store, so Abby and I rush after him.

"It's TR!" Daniel calls as soon as we get through the door. "He went that way!"

We race down the street until we see Tim Raveltere in the distance. He looks around and then heads down an alley.

"We've got him trapped," Daniel says.

"We'd better be careful," I warn. "Or he'll have us trapped."

"Let's just go slowly and quietly and see what he's up to," Abby suggests.

"Good idea," I reply.

We sneak over to the alley and Daniel leans around the corner to take a look. Luckily, Tim Raveltere's back is turned toward us, so Daniel gestures for Abby and me to come take a look.

Tim holds up his watch and taps it. The watch begins to glow, just like *The Book of Memories*, and a 3-D scene appears on the alley wall. From the hieroglyphics on the wall, we can tell it's a scene from ancient Egypt. There's a woman sitting on a golden throne.

"Cleopatra," Abby whispers. "I bet it's her. Right, Daniel?"

But Daniel doesn't say a word. His eyes are wide and he's taking everything in.

Tim Raveltere steps into the scene. He disappears, and so does the scene on the wall.

"Okay. Ancient Egypt, here we come," I say, pulling out *The Book of Memories*.

"Are you crazy?" Daniel says. "There's not enough time!"

"He's right," Abby agrees. "And there's also the fact that we have no idea exactly what time it was in that scene."

"Well, that's not exactly true," Daniel admits. "It may be possible to figure that out."

"See?" I say. "He knows we should go."

"Hey, that's not what I said," Daniel protests. "I just said that . . ."

"He said he figured out what time it was in that scene," I say. "And we know Ms. Tremt is worried. We know Tim Raveltere is up to no good. He has that pendant Ms. Tremt wanted me to leave in 1977. Who knows what he's going to do with it? We might be needed to save the world as we know it!"

"Let's not get crazy, Jada," Abby says. "He might just be an old boyfriend Ms. Tremt is trying to avoid or something."

"Maybe," I say. "But do you really want to take that chance? Because I don't."

"Do you really want to sit here wasting time arguing with Jada?" Daniel laughs. "Because you know you're not going to win that fight, Abby."

"That's for sure." Abby laughs too.

I just hope I'm not leading my friends into a fight *we* can't win.

I still don't think it's a good idea to follow Tim," Daniel says. "But there is a way to figure out exactly where he went."

"How?" Abby asks. "Are you a mind reader?"

"No," Daniel answers. "But remember— photographic memory?"

"Ahhh," I say. "That's right, boy wonder."

Let me explain. It was actually funny when Abby said that we were too busy studying to know about music, because Daniel Chang *never* studies. At least, I've never seen him study. Daniel has one of those brains where once he looks at something, it just sticks. Forever. He's kind of the reason I got the idea for the sticky notes for my brain. I know I'll never match Daniel, but I figured it was worth a try.

"I get the whole photographic memory and all," Abby says. "But you'd have to see something to remember it. Something that would tell us the exact date and time. And unless I missed something, you didn't."

"You missed something, Abby." Daniel laughs. "Actually, you missed a couple of things."

"Spill, boy wonder," Abby says.

"Sure. You definitely don't need a photographic memory to remember the first clue," Daniel begins. "Did either of you notice something interesting about the woman sitting on the throne?"

"You mean Cleopatra?" I ask.

"We can't just assume that," Daniel says. "I just finished learning about ancient Egypt in my history class. So a lot of this is still fresh in my memory. There were other female rulers in ancient Egypt. Hatshepsut, Ahhotep, Nefertiti. But there *were* clues that it was Cleopatra."

"And they are . . . ?" I ask.

"The Roman soldiers in the scene," Daniel explains. "They're Caesar's Praetorian Guard. I could tell from their armor. That means it's definitely Cleopatra sitting on the throne."

"Great," Abby says. "Continue."

"I was talking about another clue," Daniel said. "If you looked closely at the woman—at Cleopatra—you couldn't have missed it. Did you notice where her hands were?"

I close my eyes and try to remember the scene. It's pretty blurry, but I think Cleopatra's hands were folded on her stomach. Her very round stomach.

"She's pregnant!" I cry.

"Ding! Ding! Ding!" Daniel chimes. "We have a winner!"

Daniel explains that Cleopatra gave birth to the son of Julius Caesar, the Roman leader, in June in the year 47 BC.

"Let's go!" I say excitedly.

"Jada, that doesn't really change things," Daniel says. "We have an idea of where to go, but our three hours are still almost up. We need to get back home."

"Our three hours in Hollywood, 1977, are almost up," I remind him. "Ms. Tremt didn't say anything about another time and place."

"Jada, listen to me," Abby says. "I don't want to get stuck in ancient Egypt because of a guess. We have twenty-seven minutes. If we can figure out *exactly* where Tim Raveltere traveled to in the next three minutes, I'll agree to swing by there on the way home. But otherwise, no go."

"I'm pretty sure 47 BC is accurate. Cleopatra did have three other children later," Daniel explains. "But because of the guards, I'm pretty sure this is the Caesar's baby, and considering the size of her belly, I'm thinking this is sometime in the spring."

"Sometime in the spring isn't close enough, Daniel," Abby says. "We need to be precise if we want to find Tim Raveltere."

"I know," Daniel says. "That's where my photographic memory comes in. The rest you could have figured out on your own, if you were paying attention."

Daniel explains that the Egyptians had already been using a three-hundred-sixty-five-day calendar, like us, for a few thousand years at this point. In 47 BC, though, the new year started with January first for the first time, as Egyptians started to use the Roman calendar.

"The civic calendar was carved on a stone slab," Daniel continues. "The year was divided by season, and you could read the pictures on the calendar to tell the date."

"Are you going to get to the point soon?" I ask impatiently.

"Yes, ma'am." Daniel laughs. "It would be impossible for me to tell the date of the scene just by looking at the calendar. But there was a businessman there, and he was holding a scroll. I think it was a record of a tax payment, and the date was carved in the top.

"If I remember the pictures of the date correctly . . . ," Daniel says.

"And you do . . . ," Abby says.

"Then I can match it to the pictures on the calendar . . . ," Daniel continues.

"Which you can . . . ," I say.

"And figure out that the date is May 27, 47 BC," Daniel finishes.

"You really are a boy wonder," I say, impressed. "And that will get us close."

"But not close enough." Abby frowns. "We need a time."

"Then I'm guessing you didn't notice the tall pillar outside the windows?" Daniel says. "It's a shadow clock. May 27, 47 BC, four p.m."

I grab Daniel and give him a giant hug. He starts to squirm. Daniel is not very comfortable with public displays of affection, but I can't help myself.

We're going to have to fit in to ancient Egypt, and we don't have any clothing changes around, so it's magic scarf time. I pull mine out and wrap it around my neck. Daniel starts to squirm even more.

"Just bite the scarf bullet, Daniel," Abby says. "We won't tell anyone."

I pull out *The Book of Memories* and write the exact time and place on the card: *May 27, 47 BC, 4 p.m. Cleopatra's court, ancient Egypt.* Then I open the book and place it against the alley wall.

"Ready?" I say as the book starts to glow.

"Set," Abby says as it begins to swell.

"Go!" Daniel shouts as Cleopatra's court appears on the wall.

We hold hands, a lot tighter than we did before, and step into the scene. I'll admit, we're all a little scared. I can speak for my friends because their palms are sweaty, and it's kind of gross. I think it's against the rules to bring hand sanitizer to ancient Egypt, though.

We fortunately step right behind a giant stone statue, so it's pretty easy to hide out and observe. I'm going to say that gold is a definite fashion trend in ancient Egypt. There's a lot of gold in the room, and most of it is hanging off of Cleopatra. She's also obviously a fan of the dramatic eyeliner look. I have to say, it's not my style, but it is working for her.

She doesn't look anything like the pictures I've seen of her in books and at the museum. I know Cleopatra has been described as "a woman of incredible beauty," and she almost always looks like some ancient Egyptian supermodel queen in movies. The real Cleopatra is definitely pretty, but I wouldn't say that she's supermodel beautiful. It's more like an inner beauty that shows on the outside.

You can tell she's a very strong and proud woman. That's a beautiful thing. When she smiles, she looks totally friendly and charming. Everyone around her smiles back, and it's not because they're afraid of her; it's because they can't help themselves.

Her voice sounds powerful, but sweet, too. Incredibly, I understand what she's saying, even though I definitely don't know a word of ancient Egyptian. Ms. Tremt's magical scarves definitely have more power than we thought.

"Psst," Abby whispers to me. "Over there."

Tim Raveltere is dressed so absurdly we almost blow our cover and laugh out loud. He's wearing a striped head covering that flops down around his ears, gold armbands, and a white cloth wrapped around his waist. He looks pretty uncomfortable.

"He's holding the pendant," Daniel whispers.

"I wonder what he's going to do with it," I whisper back.

Then I find out. Tim whispers something to one of the guards, who takes the pendant and puts it into a small golden box. Then he places the box on a high shelf.

"Well, that's easy enough," Abby says. "Let's get the pendant and go home."

"Easy?" Daniel complains. "How can it be easy when it's up so high?"

"Your photographic memory seems to have forgotten that our friend Abby is a baller," I remind Daniel. "With a vertical jump more than two feet high."

"Maybe not quite that high without sneakers." Abby laughs. "But definitely in reach."

"Just be careful, okay?" I say. "We don't want Tim Raveltere to see your skills. He might want to use them for evil time-traveling purposes."

We wait until Cleopatra is speaking, when everyone's attention is focused on her. Then Abby drops down to her stomach and snake-crawls across the stone floor from pillar to pillar. (She doesn't have to, but I let her be dramatic because I know it makes her happy.) She waits at the last pillar until I give her the thumbs-up, letting her know the coast is clear. Then Abby jumps up, grabs the box, and takes out the pendant. Another jump and the box is back on the shelf. Abby snake-crawls her way back to us.

"Eighteen minutes to spare," Abby notes.

"Can we say thirteen?" I laugh. "I need five more minutes. There are a couple of fashion tips I want to get from Cleopatra. Look at her—she's styling!"

"Are you serious?" Daniel asks incredulously. "Are you planning to bring gold headdresses back into style?"

"Give her a break, Daniel," Abby says, acting like a bestie. "We just pulled off something amazing. Jada can get a little fashion reward."

I see one of Cleopatra's servants holding a tray with small pots and brushes.

"Makeup set, definitely," I say. "Come on, Abby. Let's go talk some fashion with a real diva."

"I'll be over there," Daniel says. "I want to check out the shadow clock up close. It's pretty cool."

Abby and I walk over to the servant.

"Cleopatra asked me to touch up her eyeliner,"

I tell the servant. "I'll need that now."

He shockingly believes me and hands me the tray. We head over to Cleopatra, bowing and waving our arms. I have no idea how to act in front of a queen, so I just try to look really humble.

"Forgive me, your line is fading," I say, dipping a brush in black dye and holding it out to the queen.

"Please, fix it," Cleopatra says.

"You are glowing with beauty," I say as I brush the eyeliner onto her eyelid.

Cleopatra smiles so brightly I have to look away.

"Thank you," she says and smooths her hair. "Is there anything else?"

"Just one little thing," I say. "Kind queen, I humbly ask your advice. I have a festival to go to next week, and I'm not sure if I should wear my hair up or down."

"Up," Cleopatra says. "Your cheekbones are striking. It will make them stand out."

"Great," I say. "And dress color? Any ideas?"

Cleopatra takes my hand and pulls me in

front of her. She looks me up and down. I realize that I have no idea what she's looking at because the scarf is cloaking me in ancient Egyptian clothing.

"Well, this shade of green is all wrong on you," Cleopatra says. "It makes you look sickly. Are you sick?"

"No!" I say. "Not at all."

Cleopatra calls to a servant, who brings over a box filled with a variety of colored fabrics. The Egyptian queen starts picking out different swatches and holding them up to me.

"She does look pretty in pink," Cleo says. She turns to Abby. "Do you agree?"

"Yes, it's a good color for her," Abby says. "But I don't think it's her best."

"No, you're right," Cleo says. "What about something metallic?"

"Ooooh, silver and gold," Abby says. "Great idea. I like it!"

At this point Daniel is pointing to the shadow clock and generally freaking out. I realize that Cleopatra could go on and on and on. I'm not sure about the silver and gold idea, but I'm going to have to end the conversation.

"I *love* that idea," I gush. "Of course, not as much gold as a queen; maybe just a little highlight of sparkle here and there."

"Exactly!" Cleopatra agrees. "Now, please, make sure my bath is ready."

"Of course!" I say, pulling Abby along.

We grab Daniel on our way and head out of the room to find a private spot where we can transport home. And that's when Tim Raveltere spots us.

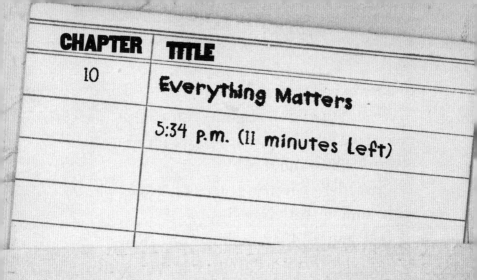

So now I'm thinking that Daniel was right—I should *not* have spent those extra five minutes talking to Cleopatra, because it looks like we're going to really need them. This is T-R-O-U-B-L-E with a capital *T*, and all the other letters too.

Tim Raveltere taps the guards and angrily points to us.

I try to wave them off, but they are clearly not taking orders from me.

Cleopatra appears behind them in the hallway.

"What does she have in her hands?" the

Egyptian queen demands. "Get it for me, now!"

The guards storm toward us. Abby starts to whimper. I can feel my heart beating so hard it might explode from my chest and fall onto the cold, stone floor. I turn to Daniel, hoping beyond hope that he will have some genius idea inspired by *Star Wars* or some other epic sci-fi movie that will save us from becoming prisoners of ancient Egypt for all time. Because if we pull our scarves off right now, in front of Cleopatra and her whole court, something even worse could happen. People would start talking about the mysterious kids who disappeared. History would change. It's just too dangerous.

"I've got you now, minions." Tim Raveltere snickers. He sounds so incredibly evil and silly at the same time that the three of us just stop and stare at him.

"Minions?" Abby says incredulously. "We're not your minions."

"No, I didn't mean *my* minions, silly girl," Tim Raveltere says. "Minions of that wacky whirlwind Valerie Tremt! Isn't that what you are? Well, she won't be able to limit time-travel continuum to her favorite students any longer. In my hands, *The Book of Memories* will transform history—the way I want it!"

My mind goes to the one place it always goes when I'm scared, or tired, or sick. *Mom. MOM!* my brain screams. *HELP!*

I focus on a psychic message and send it to her. I don't believe it will help, but I didn't believe in time travel until a day ago, either.

Mom, I don't know how you're going to fix this, but if you do, I promise I will study spelling words night and day, I swear. *I'm sorry, I'm so sorry, Mom. Just please get us out of here.*

I quietly take *The Book of Memories* out of my back pocket, because I figure we're going to need it quickly if we're going to escape. And the book starts to glow. The ten-minute warning! We have ten minutes left to get out of here, or be stuck in ancient Egypt forever.

But one of the guards spots the glowing book and starts to reach for it. Just as he's about to grab *The Book of Memories* out of my hand, Daniel pops in.

"Excuse me," Daniel says, interrupting my

thoughts as he grabs a pot off the makeup tray. "Jada, Abby, follow my lead."

Abby and I both stare blankly at him.

"Grab a pot!" Daniel yells.

I grab a pot and resign myself to the fact that I'm going to spend the rest of my days locked in a jail cell in ancient Egypt, holding a pot of kohl. If I'm lucky.

Mom . . . Mom . . . Mom . . . Mom . . . , I repeat in my head, over and over.

Then Daniel opens the pot, pours the powder into his hand, and blows into it. A cloud of black smoke begins to cover him, but not quite fully.

"COME ON!" Daniel yells.

Abby and I furiously dump our pots out and blow. While we're creating the clouds to cover us, Daniel grabs our hands and takes off his scarf.

ZLIGZAP!

Cleopatra and the guards disappear from sight. Abby, Daniel, and I are instantly transported back to the library of Sands Middle School. Luckily the library was empty except for Ms. Tremt, so nobody saw us suddenly appear.

"Well, that went well," I joke.

Abby grabs me by the shoulder and shakes me. She looks like she's about to cry.

"You . . . you . . . ," she says. "Sometimes I just can't . . ."

I don't know how to say I'm sorry, so I just give her a hug. Abby pulls Daniel into the hug too. All the worry and fear we were feeling swirls around in the hug until it just floats away and we're just relieved to be back home, together.

"Brilliant thinking, Daniel." Ms. Tremt claps from behind her desk. She has a mirror and a pot of eye makeup on her desk and is lining her eyes Cleopatra-style. It was a good look for the Egyptian queen. It is not a good look for Ms. Tremt.

"Using the powder from Cleopatra's makeup tray to hide you while you take off your scarf, revealing your 1977 clothing, which instantly brings you back to the present," Ms. Tremt continues. "Very clever indeed."

"Ms. Tremt, I still don't understand why we needed to hide when we took the scarves off," Abby said.

"Abby, it's all about trying to change as little

as possible in the past," Ms. Tremt explains. "It's one thing to just disappear or appear in front of people. It can always be laughed off as a magic trick. But it's another to leave people with a glimpse of something from the future—a piece of technology, or even clothing. That's something that may set someone's brain in motion to create something or do something differently that may change the course of history." Ms. Tremt laughs. "It sounds ridiculous, I know, but you never know what someone could get inspired to create by seeing your 1977 platform shoes!

"So now that you're back home," Ms. Tremt continues. "How was 1977?"

I want to tell Ms. Tremt about our trip, I really do. But I need a minute to catch my breath. And so do Daniel and Abby. So we grab three chairs and collapse in them.

"Here," I say, handing Ms. Tremt the pendant and *The Book of Memories*. "I know you didn't want me to bring this back to the present, but I assumed you also didn't want Tim Raveltere to have it, so I had no choice but to bring it back."

"Thank you," she replies. "I won't be able to

get this to stay in the past for long, but at least it will buy me a day or so until I can get someone else to get rid of it in time for me—permanently."

Then Ms. Tremt gets up and walks to the secret room. Through the open door, we can see a scene appear on the door. It looks like it might be some kind of samurai battle scene. There are warriors on horseback in black and red uniforms waving katana swords in the air. It definitely looks exciting, but I think Daniel, Abby, and I have had enough excitement for a while. We watch as Ms. Tremt hurls the pendant into the scene.

"She's got a pretty good arm," Daniel whispers.

"She must have gotten some tips from Matt Vezza." I laugh.

"That should give Tim something to do for a while," Ms. Tremt says, coming back into the main part of the library.

"Was it some kind of tracking device?" I ask. "That Tim Raveltere was using to find you?"

"Something like that," Ms. Tremt says quietly. "I can't reveal the details, Jada, but you're a smart girl with a logical brain, right?"

"Right," I agree. "But why did you ask me to leave it in 1977 if you could have just thrown it into time on your own?"

"Like I said, I can't reveal the details," Ms. Tremt says. "But the pendant has a boomerang effect to whomever it's locked on. It will be back before long, unless I can find someone else to deposit it for me."

"So who is this shady guy Tim Raveltere?" Abby wonders.

"I can't reveal that information either, Abby," Ms. Tremt says. "But you're right; he is shady."

"He mentioned something about wanting *The Book of Memories* for himself," I tell Ms. Tremt. "So that he could make changes in history—big changes."

"That's why the book is precious, and needs to be protected," Ms. Tremt says.

She looks shaken at the thought of Tim Raveltere's plan.

"Have you heard of the butterfly effect?" Ms. Tremt asks us.

"Not really," I reply.

"It's a theory that everything in the universe, through all of space and time, is interdependent," Ms. Tremt says. "Everything matters. One change in the initial conditions can lead to drastic results. If a butterfly flaps its wings in New Mexico, it has the power to cause a hurricane in China."

"Then how are *we* able to make one small change?" I wonder.

"It's another detail I can't go deeply into," Ms. Tremt says. "But I can tell you that as a librarian, I do my research. My selections are made with careful consideration of all the things that may happen and all the things that might not. I wouldn't put *The Book of Memories* into anyone's hands—young or old—without knowing fully the ramifications of what will happen. And that is why *The Book of Memories* was put into *my* hands."

"Who put it there?" Daniel wonders.

"Again, not information I can share," Ms. Tremt says.

She closes her eyes, and her face begins to change. Ms. Tremt always looks enthusiastic, if not happy. Now she looks sort of sad. I get the feeling that whoever put the book into Ms. Tremt's hands is no longer around.

"But *The Book of Memories* isn't the only time-travel device," Abby says. "Because Tim Raveltere traveled through time without it."

"Correct," Ms. Tremt replies. "He has a different sort of time-travel device; you might have seen him tapping it."

"The watch!" Daniel, Abby, and I shout at the same time.

"Yes, the watch," Ms. Tremt says. "It enables him to travel through time, but only *The Book of Memories* gives time travelers the ability to make a change that will stick."

"And our change was getting Tim Raveltere off your trail, right?" I ask. "That's why you didn't send me back to last week?"

Ms. Tremt pats me on the back and smiles.

"Not quite," she says. "Let's just say it was an unintended benefit."

"So there wasn't a change at all?" I wonder.

"Be patient, Jada," Ms. Tremt says. "You'll figure it out, in due time. But now I want to hear all about your trip."

I tell Ms. Tremt about Aunt Katy and Galaxian's costume studio, and how I was able to help fix Aunt Katy's sateen mistake.

"So spelling came in handy for you?" Ms. Tremt says.

"It did," I say. "I will admit that."

"Ms. Tremt," Daniel asks, "can I ask if you lived through 1977?"

"You may." Ms. Tremt laughs. "And I did."

"Can you do the Hustle?" Abby asks.

"Are you kidding?" Ms. Tremt says.

Ms. Tremt gives us back our cell phones.

"If you can find the song, I can show you in person."

Abby taps her cell phone and quickly finds the song in a music app. The chiming notes and "woo oooh ooohs" echo in the library.

"I hope you're going to join me," Ms. Tremt says.

We follow her lead as she takes four steps forward and claps, then four steps back.

We're in the middle of dancing when Mrs. Donnelly walks into the library with a group of kids.

"Are we doing the Hustle in detention now?" Mrs. Donnelly laughs. "Times have sure changed from the days when we had to write, 'I will not talk in class' one hundred times on the blackboard."

"I'm sorry," Ms. Tremt said. "I forgot you said you needed the library for detention period today. We'll be out of your way in no time."

Abby taps off the music and we head out of the room with Ms. Tremt.

"I hope you enjoyed your time travel," Ms. Tremt says to us as she shakes our hands. "I hope you enjoyed it enough to go back. Because I may need your time spy help in the future."

"Like the year 3050?" I laugh.

"Maybe not that far ahead." Ms. Tremt smiles. "For now I think some of you may have dinner plans in your immediate future."

"Dinner!" Daniel shouts. "That's why my stomach's been growling!"

Daniel, Abby, and I usually head in different directions after school, but today we decide to take the long way home and stop in the park.

"Look at those little kids on the jungle gym," Daniel says. "Imagine if we could time travel back to watch our toddler selves?"

"Can we go back in time and see our former selves?" Abby wonders. "That's a good question for Ms. Tremt. At any rate, that would be hysterical. I bet Jada would be telling all the other little kids what to do."

"Hey!" I protest. "I'm not *that* bossy! But since I already have the reputation"—I laugh—"let's head over to the swings."

"Yes, ma'am." Daniel salutes.

Sometimes when you're in middle school you look at little kid things and they seem so embarrassing. Like you can't believe you ever stumbled around a park chasing bubbles that your mom was blowing. But other times, you look at little kid things and you want to go back there, just forget about everything on your mind right now and all the things that are waiting for you in the future, and be carefree and tune out.

The very best place in the world to do that is on a swing.

Of course, the swings are pretty popular, and you don't want to look like a loser and take one away from some little kid who is waiting for a turn. We get lucky, though, and there are three empty swings, side by side, as if they are waiting for us to take our place on them.

We kick our legs out and rock back and forth, back and forth. Abby's the strongest and she's soon going faster and higher than me or

Daniel, but that's okay. For a few minutes we don't say a single word; we just swing. It feels ahhhMAZING.

"So, guys," Abby calls out to us as she swings by. "Am I the only one who was completely terrified back there?"

"No!" I shout back to her. "I was so scared all I could think about was my mom!"

"Daniel, that was so incredible, but I had no idea what you were doing," Abby admits. "I thought you were just caught in the craziness of the moment."

"Crazy is right." I laugh. "What was I thinking, talking to Cleopatra about dresses for the dance?"

"You are crazy, girl," Abby says. "Crazy for fashion."

"You know it," I reply.

The three of us haven't been friends for very long. We went to different elementary schools, so we just met last year in sixth grade. Don't get me wrong. We hang out all the time, and when we're not together we're always texting or doing group chats with one another. But now, with everything we just experienced time traveling, I think our friendship has reached a new level. I think we'll always have ancient Egypt and 1977, and it will always keep us close, no matter where we go to high school, or college, or off into the world after that.

"Are you two busy on Saturday?" I ask.

"I have a basketball game in the evening," Abby says. "But I'm free before that."

"Me too," Daniel says. "What's going on?"

"I have a favor to ask," I tell them. "And I want some company."

"Please, don't tell me it's another trip through time." Daniel groans.

"No, it's not," I say with a laugh. "At least not in a *Book of Memories* time-travel way."

"Then I'm in," Daniel says.

"Me too," Abby agrees.

"Great," I say. "My house at ten, Saturday morning."

There's a shortcut I always take home from the park, but I don't take it today. I'd rather walk with Abby and Daniel and spend a few more minutes with them. I'm not sure if I even look or sound normal, and I'm a little worried Mom is going to know that something happened in school today. Mother's instinct, and all that.

At home, I walk upstairs and find Mom in her room, folding laundry.

"What took you so long?" Mom asks. "You're usually home before I am."

"Didn't you get my text?" I say. "I said I was going to stop at the park on the way home."

"I got it," Mom says. "I just didn't think you'd be there that long. Is everything okay?"

"Not really, actually," I say.

And then the tears start and I fall apart a little.

"Oh, Jada," Mom says. "What's the matter, honey?"

Her voice is so warm it wraps me up and cuddles me, just like her arms are doing right now. I stay inside her hug until I'm all cried out.

"Just a rough day," I say.

Then I pull out my progress report.

"And there's this," I say, holding it out to her and sniffling.

"Okay, Jada," Mom says. "Let's talk."

"I know," I say. "I'm sorry I'm such a disappointment."

I'm swooped up in a Mom hug again.

"Jada, how can you say that?" Mom says. "You're never a disappointment. You're remarkable. But you're not perfect. . . . No one is.

"Look," she continues. "Running away from your problems is a race you'll never win. You may never win the spelling bee. But if you decide that spelling is important and you put some effort in—all the time, not just when you fail a test— you might be the change you'd like to see."

"Oh, Mom." I groan. "That was not good."

"I know." Mom laughs. "But you need a plan, Jada. A serious plan. And you need to stick to it."

"I know," I say. "And I know you're always there to help."

"And I always will be." Mom smiles. "Now, let's go downstairs and get dinner started."

Whenever I'm feeling bad, Mom and Dad always whip up the perfect food to make me feel better. Tonight it's going to be meat loaf with creamy mashed potatoes and string beans on the side. My stomach's already growling.

"Do you like Earth, Wind, and Fire?" I ask Mom while I'm peeling potatoes with Dad.

Mom laughs. "How do you know about Earth, Wind, and Fire?"

"Oh, someone was playing it in the park," I fib. "And I asked them who it was because I kind of liked it."

"My mom used to listen to them over and over," Mom says. "It got pretty annoying after a while. Or at least that's how I felt back then."

"Remember those wild outfits our parents used to wear?" Dad adds.

"I sure do," Mom says. "I think I have some of them in boxes up in the attic that Mom gave me in case we wanted them for that Halloween party. Even though I'd like to forget some of them."

"I think we also have some of those photos from my dad's house," says Dad. "And you have that incredible one of your mom outside the record store."

"I want to see!" Sam cries.

"After dinner," Dad tells him. "Go finish your homework; dinner will be ready soon."

At dinner I gobble up two slices of meat loaf and a mound of mashed potatoes so big it nearly falls off my plate. Then I ask for seconds.

"You must be getting ready for a growth spurt," Dad says. "I've never seen you eat that much before."

"Maybe," I say. "Or I used up a lot of energy running around today."

"It's just a park." Mom laughs. "You used to run around there for hours, Jada."

If she only knew.

After Sam and I clear the table and load the dishes into the dishwasher, Mom gets out the old photo albums. Sam giggles and screams at how young our grandparents were and the crazy clothing they were wearing. I'm not surprised.

"Nice poncho, Grandpa." I laugh. "And Grandma is rocking that maxi dress."

"How do you know about ponchos and maxi dresses?" Dad asks.

"There was a seventies tribute in one of the blogs I read," I bluff. "It had links to music and fashion of the times. Soooo groovy!"

Mom pulls one large eight-by-ten photo

from a big stained envelope.

"This is my favorite picture of my mother of all time," Mom says. "I *cannot* believe she ever left the house looking like this."

I take the photo from Mom's hands and smile. It's Gran, aka Brenda, standing outside of Crane's, in her crop top, denim skirt, and silver boots.

"I think she looks fabulous," I say. "I love her style."

"You might be the only one, Jada." Dad laughs. "Those boots are an abomination."

"Dad!" I shout. "You should never, ever give anyone fashion advice. Those boots are the *best*!

"Can I keep this picture, Mom?" I ask. "I might use it as inspiration for some of my fashion designs."

"Of course," Mom says as she puts the photo back into the envelope and hands it to me. "But you better take a shower and get ready for bed. You look exhausted."

"Not without studying spelling!" I say seriously. "And tonight I want you to give me forty words, not twenty!"

Mom rubs her eyes and blinks, then looks at my dad.

"Are you hearing what I'm hearing?" she asks him. "Tell me I'm not dreaming."

"I am, and you're not," Dad says.

"You never know when one word can make all the difference," I explain.

"That's what I've been trying to tell you!" Mom cries.

"And I wasn't really listening," I admit. "But now I know you were right. So let's study."

Luckily, Mom is ahead of me on the stairs when she says, "You know, I remember hearing a story about your Aunt Katy. She nearly lost her internship at the movie studio once because of one misspelled word. And who knows what might have happened then. She may never have opened her own design studio!"

If I had been sitting on the couch next to Mom when she said that, I would not have been able to hide my true feelings. Which are . . .

WOOOOO-HOOOOOO! Aunt Katy has her own studio!

I did it! I made *one small change*! I helped

Aunt Katy's biggest dream come true. Before my trip to the past she was just a buyer for a store. I bet she's designing her very own clothes, not for actresses but for "girls who look like us." Yes, yes, yes! Yay, Aunt Katy!

I give a little fist pump to myself and then try to compose myself.

"It's funny how she and I both love fashion—and we both have trouble with spelling," I tell my mom.

"Yes, it might be a coincidence," Mom says. "Or it could be DNA."

"Do you *ever* stop being a science teacher, Mom?" I laugh.

"Sure," Mom replies. "Why don't you try spelling *coincidence*?"

"C-O-W-I-N . . . ," I start.

"Let's get back to that one." Mom laughs. "How about *DNA*?"

"Mom!" I yell, chasing after her as she runs up the stairs away from me, still laughing. "That's just mean!"

CHAPTER	TITLE
12	Everybody, Dance Now!

I can't wait to tell Ms. Tremt the news about Aunt Katy (even though she probably already knows), so the next morning I head to school a little early, throw my books into my locker, and head straight for the library. I reach down and grab the door handle, but it won't turn.

Which is weird, because the library door is never locked. I put my ear to the door and hear rustling noises inside. My heart starts to pound. Has Tim Raveltere tracked Ms. Tremt back to Sands Middle School? Did we do something wrong? Is all of time going to be put in his evil hands because he's stolen *The Book of Memories?*

While I'm crouched down with my ear to the door, it suddenly swings open and I tumble to the ground. I look up and see Luis Ramirez and his friend Patrick McMann staring at me.

"Were you looking for something?" Luis asks, trying to hide a smile.

"Um, is Ms. Tremt around?" I ask awkwardly.

"Yup, she's in there," Patrick says.

I stand up and stare deeply into Luis's eyes. I know I'm not allowed to talk to him about the whole time travel thing, but I figure that maybe I can kind of give him a look that says, *Hey, I know where you're coming from; I was just there too,* and also, *We have more in common than you think, dude.*

Luis just looks back at me blankly. He definitely did not receive that message.

"Come on, Patrick. We'd better get going," Luis says nervously. "See you later, Jada."

They start to walk away from me and I can hear them both crack up laughing. I mean, I'm sure it was funny when I fell on the floor and all, but it wasn't *that* funny.

Then Patrick puts his arm around Luis's shoulder and says, "Dude, she seriously is in love with you. Did you see the way she was staring into your eyes?"

OMG! I want to scream down the hallway at them, *I am* NOT *in love with Luis. I am not in love with anyone! I just wanted him to know that I know what he knows and that I'm okay with him knowing that I know it too.*

But I don't. Because that would look totally pathetic and probably not even make sense. I also want to shout, *Hello, "she" is only two feet away from you. Maybe you should try whispering instead of blurting it out so she can hear every embarrassing word that you're saying!*

I don't say that either, though. I figure Abby will be able to straighten it out somehow. She lives down the street from Luis, and they've been friends since they were chasing after bubbles together as little kids.

I walk into the library and see Ms. Tremt sitting at her desk. Her brow is furrowed and she looks nervous and worried as she rummages through a pile of books. I lean over to check out the titles. *The Pirate Hunter. Treasure and Intrigue. Buccaneers Who Ravaged the Seas.*

"Is someone doing a history report on pirates?" I ask. "Or visiting one in person?"

Ms. Tremt jumps in her seat. She didn't even see me leaning over to read the book titles. Strange.

"Jada!" Ms. Tremt says. "You're in early. Did you need something?"

"I needed to tell you about Aunt Katy," I say. "I thought you stopped my chance to make one small change when you sent me to 1977 instead of last week's spelling test. I thought that you wanted me to make the change for you. But you didn't. At all. You knew there was a better choice."

"I wouldn't say 'knew,'" Ms. Tremt corrects me. "I just had a moment of inspiration, perhaps."

"Well, it was an inspired idea," I tell her. "I found out last night that Aunt Katy's lifelong dream has come true now. She has her own fashion studio. And that must have happened because she didn't get fired when she was an intern in 1977. And she didn't get fired because I helped her see the misspelled word on her paper! So you gave me the chance to give Aunt Katy the one thing she always wanted. Thank you."

"You are welcome, Jada Reese," Ms. Tremt says. "And again, I will thank you for helping with my little, um, problem."

"Where is your little problem, anyway?" I ask.

"I don't know exactly," Ms. Tremt says. "I've been receiving some signs, and they aren't good, but I think I have a short-term plan for diverting Tim's attention from Sands Middle School."

"Oh, does that mean you've chosen your next time travelers?" I ask.

"I have an idea," Ms. Tremt replies.

"Of course you do, Ms. Tremt," I say. "And if you need any help, you know who to call."

"Indeed I do, Jada," Ms. Tremt says. "Now, if there isn't anything else, I'd like to get back to working on my plans, if you don't mind."

"I don't mind," I say. "But there are just a couple of other things I need."

"And they are . . . ?" Ms. Tremt asks.

"May I please borrow *How to Spell Your Way to the T-O-P?*" I ask. "And any other spelling books you have? That would be great."

Ms. Tremt gets up, scurries around the shelves, and pulls a stack of books together. It's actually impressive to watch. She didn't have to go on the computer and look them up, or dig around at all. She knew exactly where to find them.

"Here you go, Jada," Ms. Tremt says as she drops the stack of spelling books into my arms. "Is that it?"

"One more thing," I say. "Could I also borrow the clothes that Daniel, Abby, and I wore back to 1977? Just for the weekend? I promise no one will know about where we went in them."

"I think that would be okay," Ms. Tremt says.

She unlocks the secret room, rummages around in the clothing box, and puts our outfits into a paper bag.

"Have fun!" Ms. Tremt says. "And good luck with spelling!"

"Thank you!" I call back to her. "For everything!"

The rest of the week Mom and I spend one hour together before bedtime going over the books

Ms. Tremt gave me and reviewing spelling words for my next exam. I'm determined to get a good grade.

On Friday my hard work is put to the test. I don't feel as panicked as I usually do when Mr. Wiley starts to recite the list of words, but I don't feel calm and cool either. It's more a nervous butterflies-in-the-pit-of-my stomach kind of feeling. The feeling starts to go away when I recognize the first three words and spell them without having to second—and third—and fourth—guess myself.

At the end of class, Mr. Wiley asks me to stay for a minute.

"Jada, I usually wait until the weekend to grade the test," Mr. Wiley says. "But you looked a lot more comfortable than usual taking this one, so I thought I'd check to see how you did."

"And . . . ?" I ask, crossing my fingers and toes. *Please, please, please,* I think to myself.

"See for yourself," he says.

Eighty-two! I jump up and down and hug the paper.

"Thank you, Mr. Wiley," I cheer. "It's the first

time I've gotten above a seventy on a spelling test this year!"

"Yes, Jada, I grade your papers, so I already know that." Mr. Wiley laughs. "I'm glad you figured out a way to solve the problem."

And Mr. Wiley's right, I did. I was always trying to make spelling be like math and follow logical rules. And then I would get frustrated and confused. But once I got it through my head that spelling isn't like math at all, and I just needed to study harder, I finally got it.

Mr. Wiley smiles at me. "Have a good weekend, Jada," he says.

"You too!" I say. "And this weekend isn't going to be good. It's going to be GREAT!"

The weekend does start off on a good note. Mom is really proud of me when I tell her about my latest spelling test. I'm going to try for a ninety next time. She might even buy me a puppy then!

On Saturday morning at 10:02 the doorbell rings and Abby and Daniel are waiting for me.

"Did you three have plans today?" Dad asks as he flips some pancakes.

"Mom said Aunt Katy was coming over," I reply. "I thought it would be fun for us to hang out with her this afternoon."

"You did?" Dad says, blinking. "Is this for a school project? Do you need to interview a family member or something?"

"Something like that," I say. "Mom, is she coming?"

"Of course." Mom laughs. "It's Saturday morning. Gran's home soaking her beans and then mopping the floors, so Aunt Katy was stopping there first and then heading over here.

"I'm sure she'll be very happy to help," Mom says. "And to see you."

Abby and Daniel follow me to my room, and I toss the brown paper bag onto my bed.

"Do I really have to wear those clothes again?" Daniel complains.

"You do," I say. "I'm the boss, remember?"

"I think it's going to be fun," Abby says. "And I downloaded all the songs, so we're all ready."

Aunt Katy bursts through the front door and runs up the stairs to join us. With a smile she hands Mom a large pot.

"Beans, from Mom," she says.

"Gee, thanks." Mom laughs. "Can never have enough of those."

Aunt Katy doesn't look superfly, but she is still super-stylish. White linen trousers, a navy fitted blazer, light gray button shirt casually unbuttoned at the bottom and top, and a smattering of gold jewelry.

"Daniel, Abby, it's nice to see you again," Aunt Katy says. "Are you three working on a project?"

The three of us look at each other and laugh.

"Yes," I say. "We're always working on projects. And we wanted to show some of it to you."

I ask Mom if she would mind if we look around the attic.

"It's a mess up there, Jada," Mom says. "What are you looking for?"

I tell her that I'm working on some new fashion designs that are inspired by clothes from the 1970s.

"You're just like your aunt." Mom smiles. "Always drawing and designing. Keep at it—look at how far she got!"

Abby giggles.

We all head upstairs, and Daniel helps Mom pull down the attic stairs. It is a mess up there, but a mess of memories, and it's filled with good feelings. Mom's graduation gown is hanging in one corner, Dad's old basketball hoop is in another, and in between are boxes and boxes and boxes of stuff.

"I don't know where to start, Jada," Mom says. "But if you want to dig around, go right ahead. Aunt Katy and I will be in the kitchen—with Gran's beans."

Daniel opens a box and it's filled with dolls. Abby opens another and finds Mom's high school notebooks. We stop to page through them and it's like looking at a side of Mom I never knew she had. I knew Mom was a good student, but it looks like she may have had a little trouble focusing at times. My mom's name is Keisha and there are scribbles and doodles around every inch of her school notes. There are also a few interesting "Keisha Loves Matt," "Keisha Loves Rodney," "Keisha Loves Derek" notes. Interesting because my dad's name is Marcus.

We go through so many boxes and find so

many things, but not one of them has what I'm looking for. I'm just about ready to give up and move on with the rest of the plan when Abby yells over from the other side of the attic.

"Check it out!" she calls, holding up a big brown floppy suede hat. "I think I've struck gold!"

Daniel and I rush over as Abby starts to pull pants and shirts from the box. They are all straight from the 70s, and totally cool. I put on the hat and a brown suede fringed vest I find in the box.

"How do I look?" I ask as I pose.

"Funky!" Daniel laughs.

We dig to the bottom of that box, and then another, but still no luck. Aunt Katy and Mom come back up to see what all the commotion is about. They start to laugh when they see me wearing the suede hat and vest, and Abby in a dashiki and love beads.

"I see you found what you're looking for," Mom says.

"Actually, we didn't," I tell her. "I'm looking for something specific."

"What is it?" Aunt Katy asks.

I pull out the envelope with Gran's photo and show it to her. Aunt Katy smiles.

"I'm looking for these," I say, pointing to her silver boots.

"You should have told me that, Jada." Mom laughs. "Do you think I would have put *those* boots in just any old box? They're special—awfully special!"

"'Awful' being the key word." Aunt Katy laughs.

"Could I try them on?" I ask. "Just once."

"Sure," Mom says.

"Okay, let's go back downstairs," I suggest. "There's something we want to show you."

Daniel and Abby help me put all the clothes back into the boxes and stack the boxes back up neatly.

Back downstairs I hand Daniel his outfit all folded up.

"You go into the bathroom and change," I tell him. "Abby and I will wait here."

"We'll meet you in the kitchen, Aunt Katy," I call to her. "Just don't lose those boots!"

"Never!" Aunt Katy laughs back. "They're my mother's most prized possession—next to her children, of course. Although sometimes I think she loves the boots more!"

Daniel heads into the bathroom to change.

I hand Abby the polyester pants and smock top she wore to 1977. She takes the top but hands the pants back to me. Then she picks up the hat and the vest I was just wearing.

"I'm going make some changes to that outfit," she tells me. "If you don't mind."

Abby pulls out a brown suede fringed skirt from the paper bag.

"Found this in the attic," she says. "Thought I'd save it for later. Do you think your mom will mind?"

"She won't," I say. "Let's see."

The smock top looks better with the skirt, vest, and hat than it did with the polyester pants.

"Supercute!" I say. "I'm sorry Ms. Tremt didn't have something like that in her box."

"Me too." Abby laughs.

When we're finished getting dressed, we knock on the bathroom door. Daniel opens it and comes out, wearing his wide-leg corduroys and striped shirt.

"Are you ready to boogie?" I ask him.

"Now or never, Jada," he replies.

Mom and Aunt Katy are sitting on kitchen stools drinking coffee and chatting when we get to the kitchen.

"Are you ready, ladies?" I call out. "Because we are here to party!"

"Jada Reese, you are something," Aunt Katy says, shaking her head. "Where did you get that dress? It definitely wasn't up in the attic."

"Oh, I got this in school," I tell her. "At a . . . um . . . a clothing drive."

Aunt Katy makes Abby, Daniel, and me twirl around so she can get a good look at us. Abby sets up her portable speaker on the kitchen counter and plugs it into her phone.

"Whenever you're ready," she calls to me.

"Can I try on the boots now?" I ask Mom.

"Of course, honey," she says. She hands me the boots. "I keep them in a special box in the back of my closet," she says. "If you ever want them again, just ask me."

Mom hands the boots to me and I hold them like precious jewels. They look sharp, but they're so soft and smooth. I can't wait to zip them up and strut around the kitchen in them. There's just one problem. . . . They don't fit.

"I'm like a stepsister!" I moan. "Why can't I be Cinderella?"

"You can't be Cinderella because you got your father's big feet." Aunt Katy laughs. "Mine are much more ladylike."

Aunt Katy sits down and slips her foot into the left boot. It zips up easily.

"See?" she says.

"Oh, put them on!" I cry. "Please, for me?"

"We brought music," Abby says as she taps the phone screen.

Thelma Houston begins to sing.

"Hold that," Aunt Katy says.

"Yes," Mom adds. "We'll be right back."

Mom grabs the other silver boot and she heads into her bedroom with Aunt Katy. We hear them rattling through drawers and closets, and a few minutes later the sound of boot heels echoes through the hallway.

And then my mother and her big sister walk into the kitchen looking like they just stepped onto the stage of *Soul Train*. Aunt Katy is wearing a superfly, floral-print maxi dress with her silver boots. Mom has on mustard-colored bell-bottoms with a shimmery gold shirt.

"I can still bust a move, you know," Aunt Katy says. "So what are you waiting for, girl?"

Abby taps the phone screen and Thelma Houston begins to sing again.

"No, no," I call out. "Something else."

I walk over to Abby and whisper in her ear. She taps the screen a few more times and then lines up between Daniel and me. Aunt Katy looks at us, confused and amused.

The notes chime. The bass begins to thump. Maracas rattle.

Wooo, ooooh ooooh ooooh ooooh.

"Do the Hustle!" Aunt Katy shouts.

And, of course, we all do.

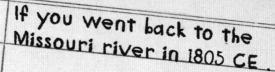

If you went back to the
Missouri river in 1805 CE...

You would find Sacagawea helping Meriwether Lewis and William Clark explore the land President Thomas Jefferson had bought in the Louisiana Purchase in 1803. Sacagawea was a Shoshone woman who spoke both her native language and English. Her skills as a translator were extremely helpful to the explorers. Her knowledge of the land was as well. She also helped ease the tension between the explorers and the Native Americans they encountered.

Two months before starting the journey,

Sacagawea gave birth to her son Jean Baptiste Charbonneau. (William Clark became the baby's godfather.) She and her husband, Toussaint Charbonneau, took the baby when they headed west with Lewis and Clark on April 7, 1805. Sacagawea did know how to identify roots, plants, and berries that could be eaten or used as medicine. While her husband received 320 acres of land and $500.33 for his service, Sacagawea got nothing.

If you went back to Hollywood, California, in 1977 . . .

If you could actually visit Hollywood, California, in 1977, you might run into a movie star or two, and you'd hear the music and see a lot of the things that Jada, Abby, and Daniel did. The fashions they picked out from Ms. Tremt's box represented the clothes of the time, and Aunt Katy and Gran Brenda were definitely dressed in clothes that were popular back then.

There were two record stores called Crane's in Los Angeles, but they were in the Inglewood and Palos sections, not Hollywood. Going to the record store wasn't just a quick shopping trip, but an event. They were more than just stores; they were places to hang out and check out the latest trends in music and styles.

There were several major movie studios in Hollywood, California, in 1977, and there still are today, and Paul Newman, Sally Field, and Sidney Poitier were all popular actors at the time. Galaxian Studios is completely fictional, though it does represent the things you'd find in a typical studio—sets, props, costumes, and yes, catering service with cookies.

If you went back to Egypt in 47 BCE . . .

You would find Cleopatra on the throne, as she was queen of Egypt, Cyprus, and Cyrene from 51 BCE, when she inherited the throne with her brother, to her death in 30 BCE.

When the Roman leader Julius Caesar landed with a small group of troops in Alexandria, Cleopatra's brother Ptolemy tried to convince him to name him as sole ruler of Egypt. Cleopatra snuck into the palace to see Caesar and persuaded him to support her instead. She and Julius Caesar did have a son, named Caesarion, who was born on June 23, 47 BCE.

The ancient Egyptians thought that beauty was a sign of holiness, and believed the pharaoh was a link between the world of the gods and the world of humans. Therefore makeup and fashion were indeed an important part of Cleopatra's world. In some Egyptian tombs, makeup trays were buried with the dead.

The classic thick black eyeliner seen in ancient Egyptian art was created by kohl. Powdered kohl was created by grinding up minerals. Another powdered dye, henna, was created from crushing the leaves of a shrub.

The ancient Egyptians were one of the first people to keep time by dividing the day into equal parts, and they used sundials and shadow clocks to tell time.

When Luis Ramirez gets a chance to go back in time, he knows just what he wants to do. He plans to go back to 1696 and see where Captain Kidd left buried treasure, and then retrieve it. But when he brags about time travel to his older brother Rafael, he doesn't believe him. Luis decides there's only one way to convince him—he'll bring *The Book of Memories* home to show him. Sure, the book is a time portal, but it's still only a book. What could go possibly go wrong? Turns out—a lot!